STORIES IN TIME

OUR WORLD'S STORY

ACTIVITY BOOK

TEACHER'S EDITION

HARCOURT BRACE & COMPANY

Orlando Atlanta Austin Boston San Francisco Chicago Dallas

New York Toronto London

For permission to reprint copyrighted material, grateful acknowledgment is made to the following sources:

Doubleday, a division of Bantam Doubleday Dell Publishing Group, Inc.: From *Alexander of Macedon: The Journey to World's End* by Harold Lamb. Text copyright 1946 by Harold Lamb.

Oberlin College Press: From "Five Hundred Words About My Journey from the Capital to Feng-Hsien" by Tu Fu and from "Fighting South of the Ramparts" by Li Po in *Five T'ang Poets*, translated by David Young, Vol. 15 from *The Field Translation Series*. Published in 1990.

Twayne Publishers, an imprint of Simon & Schuster Macmillan: From *Tu Fu* by A. R. Davis. Text copyright © 1971 by Twayne Publishers, Inc.

Zondervan Publishing House: Scripture from the *New Revised Standard Version Bible*. Text copyright 1989 by the Division of Christian Education of the National Council of the Churches of Christ in the U.S.A.

Printed in the United States of America

ISBN 0-15-307923-1

2 3 4 5 6 7 8 9 10 085 99 98 97

The activities in this book reinforce or extend social studies concepts and skills in **OUR WORLD'S STORY.** There is one activity for each lesson and skill. Reproductions of the activity pages appear with answers in the Teacher's Edition.

CONTENTS

NAME _____ DATE _____

What's in a WORD?

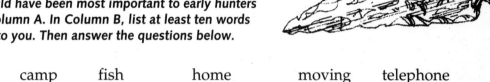

Make Comparisons

DIRECTIONS: Look at the words in the box below. List at least
ten words that would have been most important to early hunters
and gatherers in Column A. In Column B, list at least ten words
that are important to you. Then answer the questions below.

basketball	camp	fish	home	moving	telephone
bed	cave	food	homework	school	television
bison	family	friends	hunting	spear	water

COLUMN A		COLUMN B	
bison	friends	basketball	home
camp	hunting	bed	homework
cave	moving	family	school
family	spear	food	telephone
fish	water	friends	television
food		water	

1. What does the list in Column A tell you about the lives of hunters and gatherers?
Survival took up most of their time and energy. The clan was important.
_____

2. What does the list in Column B tell you about our society today?
We have time for leisure and entertainment, but we must still meet our basic needs to survive.
_____

3. Which words appear in both lists? Explain your answer. Students should list food and
water and perhaps family and friends. Basic human physical and emotional needs do not change.
_____

Slash-and-Burn farming

The slash-and-burn method of farming was used by some early peoples. Today it is widely used in the Amazon rain forest and other tropical forests.

Form a Sequence

DIRECTIONS: Read the six steps involved in slash-and-burn farming. Then number the illustrations to correctly match the descriptions.

1. Small trees and vegetation are cut down.

2. When the plants have dried in the sun, the area is burned.

3. Seeds are planted in the ashes.

4. Crops are grown for several years.

5. When the nutrients in the soil are used up, farmers move to another place to start over.

6. If left undisturbed, the forest grows back. After many years the land may be farmed again.

Use after reading Chapter 1, Lesson 2, pages 44–47.

Harcourt Brace School Publishers

HOW TO READ A PARALLEL TIME LINE

Apply Time Line Skills

DIRECTIONS: The three-part time line on page 4 shows what was happening in different areas of life in the United States in the twentieth century. Use the time line to answer the questions below.

1. What could kids do for fun in 1960? play with toys such as the Hula Hoop™, the Slinky™, Silly Putty™, and Barbie dolls™; go to movies; watch TV

2. Do you think most fans who attended the first Rose Bowl game traveled in cars?

No; the first Rose Bowl game was played in 1902. The Model T, the first popular car, was introduced in 1908.

3. What might a sixth grader have played with at the time of the Persian Gulf War?

in-line skates, skateboards, or video games

4. Was racial integration first achieved in sports or in schools?

It was first achieved in sports. Jackie Robinson played major league baseball in 1947. Public schools were desegregated after 1954.

5. Which event could Americans have watched on TV in 1969?

United States astronaut Neil Armstrong walking on the moon

6. Do you think many people living today remember when Hawaii became a state?

Yes, many do. Hawaii became a state in 1959.

(Continued)

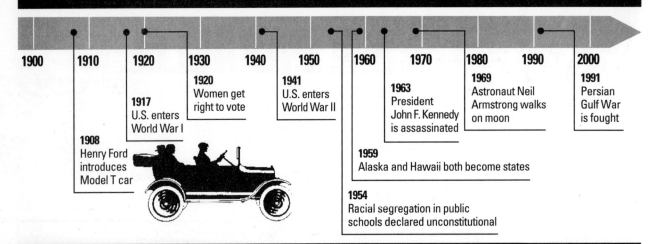

UNITED STATES MAJOR EVENTS TIME LINE, 1900–PRESENT

1900 1910 1920 1930 1940 1950 1960 1970 1980 1990 2000

1920 Women get right to vote

1941 U.S. enters World War II

1963 President John F. Kennedy is assassinated

1969 Astronaut Neil Armstrong walks on moon

1991 Persian Gulf War is fought

1917 U.S. enters World War I

1908 Henry Ford introduces Model T car

1959 Alaska and Hawaii both become states

1954 Racial segregation in public schools declared unconstitutional

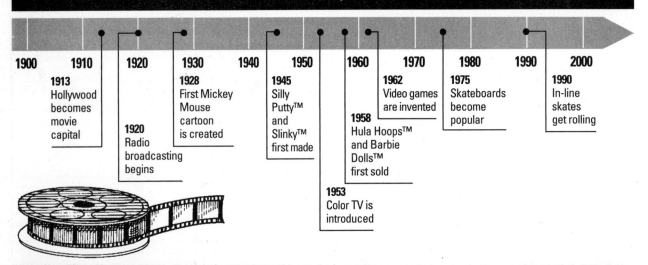

UNITED STATES ENTERTAINMENT TIME LINE, 1900–PRESENT

1900 1910 1920 1930 1940 1950 1960 1970 1980 1990 2000

1913 Hollywood becomes movie capital

1920 Radio broadcasting begins

1928 First Mickey Mouse cartoon is created

1945 Silly Putty™ and Slinky™ first made

1962 Video games are invented

1975 Skateboards become popular

1990 In-line skates get rolling

1958 Hula Hoops™ and Barbie Dolls™ first sold

1953 Color TV is introduced

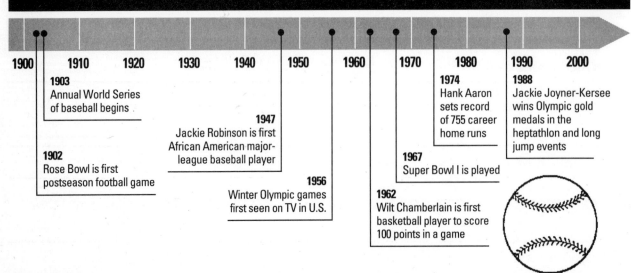

UNITED STATES SPORTS TIME LINE, 1900–PRESENT

1900 1910 1920 1930 1940 1950 1960 1970 1980 1990 2000

1903 Annual World Series of baseball begins

1947 Jackie Robinson is first African American major-league baseball player

1974 Hank Aaron sets record of 755 career home runs

1988 Jackie Joyner-Kersee wins Olympic gold medals in the heptathlon and long jump events

1902 Rose Bowl is first postseason football game

1956 Winter Olympic games first seen on TV in U.S.

1967 Super Bowl I is played

1962 Wilt Chamberlain is first basketball player to score 100 points in a game

Harcourt Brace School Publishers

A PICTURE OF DAILY LIFE

When the village of Skara Brae was uncovered on an island off northern Scotland in 1850, the well-preserved ruins provided a good picture of how people had lived there.

Draw Conclusions

DIRECTIONS: Study the drawings below of things uncovered at Skara Brae. What do they tell you? Using only the evidence of the drawings, answer the questions below.

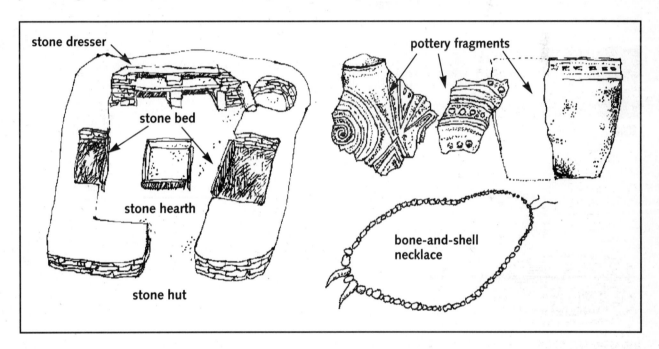

1. What material was abundant on the island? How do you know?

stone; because the hut, beds, and dresser were all made of stone

_____

2. What clue can you find about the cool temperature of the island's climate?

The hearth had beds on two sides and was in the center of the hut.

_____

3. Give two examples of evidence that the people of Skara Brae had some leisure time.

decorated pottery and necklace beads

_____

Harcourt Brace School Publishers

HOW TO MAKE A Generalization

Apply Thinking Skills

DIRECTIONS: *Below, a generalization has been made for you. Find information in your text to support the generalization, and write it on the lines below.*

Generalization:
People in early societies had to work together.

1. Hunters: Groups of hunters needed teamwork to hunt large game animals. (See PE p. 11.)

_____

_____

_____

_____

2. Early farmers: To provide for the needs of a large clan, some members had to grow or gather

food, while others made tools and clothing. (See PE p. 14.)

_____

_____

_____

3. The village of Skara Brae: In Skara Brae everyone worked together to build houses for all. Men

gathered large stones for foundations and walls. Women and children gathered smaller stones.

(See PE p. 30.)

_____

_____

_____

Use after reading Chapter 1, Skill Lesson, page 57.

People of the STONE AGE

Connect Main Ideas

DIRECTIONS: Use this organizer to show that you understand how the chapter's main ideas are connected. Complete the organizer by writing three important details about hunters and gatherers and three important details about early farmers.

Hunters and Gatherers

Early people lived and worked in groups to collect food.

1. Students may mention clans, the need to work together and the consequences of lack of cooperation, the
2. development of division of labor, and the responsibility of leaders for controlling food resources.
3. _____

People of the Stone Age

Early Farmers

Many early people became food producers instead of food collecters.

1. Students may mention geographic areas of earliest agriculture, reasons for development of agriculture,
2. and effects of changing from food collectors to food producers.
3. _____

Use after reading Chapter 1, pages 38–59.

NAME _____ DATE _____

Sumerian CULTURE

What did people need to build a civilization like Sumer, with 200,000 people living together? One thing that was very important was written language.

Decipher a Code

DIRECTIONS: *Imagine you are an archaeologist who has discovered the secret library of King Ashurbanipal of Assyria. Study these cuneiform symbols to decipher the writings.*

WA sound		WH sound	
L sound		symbol for plural	
ER sound		T sound	
Ē sound		AW sound	

DIRECTIONS: *On the first row of lines below each set of symbols, write the sounds the symbols represent. Then on the second row of lines, write the word as it would be spelled in English. The correct number of spaces is provided for you.*

WA L S̲

W A L L S

WH Ē L S

W H E E L S

WA T ER

W A T E R

WH Ē T

W H E A T

L AW S̲

L A W S

Use after reading Chapter 2, Lesson 1, pages 61–66.

The Code of
HAMMURABI

Hammurabi believed his laws would bring peace and security to the people of Babylon. By making rules and punishments that were the same throughout Babylon, he hoped to make an honest society and prevent the strong from taking advantage of the weak.

Use Source Material

DIRECTIONS: Some of Hammurabi's laws are given below. Read them carefully. Then follow the directions on the next page.

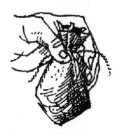

On Stealing
- 14. If a man has stolen a child, he shall be put to death.
- 22. If a man has committed highway robbery and has been caught, that man shall be put to death.

On Farming

- 42. If a man has rented a field to cultivate and has not grown any grain on the field, he shall be held responsible for not doing the work and shall pay rent.
- 48. If a man owes a debt and a storm has flooded his field or destroyed his crop, in that year he shall pay nothing.

On Harming Others
- 196. If a man has knocked out the eye of a nobleman, his eye shall be knocked out.
- 198. If a man has knocked out the eye of a poor man, he shall pay one mina of silver. (A mina equals about two pounds.)
- 200. If a nobleman has knocked out the tooth of a man who is his equal, his tooth shall be knocked out.
- 201. If a nobleman has knocked out the tooth of a poor man, he shall pay one-third of a mina of silver.

(Continued)

NAME _____ DATE _____

DIRECTIONS: Read the statements below. Underline True or
False to show whether each statement agrees with what you have
learned of Hammurabi's laws. Explain your answers.

1. Stealing was not a very serious crime.

True/False Thieves were put to death. _____

_____

_____

2. Farmers were treated fairly.

True/False It seems fair not to punish a farmer if a crop was lost through no fault of his own,

such as from bad weather. It seems fair to have to pay rent to the owner of the field if the farmer

had no crop just because the farmer was lazy.

_____

3. Laws against harming others were fair if they involved people within the same class.

True/False Law 200 shows that people in the same class were treated the same way.

_____

_____

4. Laws against harming others favored the poor.

True/False They favored the rich. People who injured the upper classes had to pay by suffering

the same injury. People who injured the poor only had to pay money.

_____

_____

Use after reading Chapter 2, Lesson 2, pages 67–71.

Harcourt Brace School Publishers

King Solomon's
TRADE AGREEMENT

About 960 B.C. King Solomon decided to build a magnificent temple. The First Book of Kings in the Bible tells how he went about it.

Use Source Material

DIRECTIONS: Read the following quotations. Then answer the questions on the next page.

"Now King Hiram of Tyre sent his servants to Solomon, when he heard that they had anointed him king in place of his father; for Hiram had always been a friend to David. Solomon sent word to Hiram, saying, . . . 'I intend to build a house for the name of the Lord my God, as the Lord said to my father David. . . . Therefore command that cedars from the Lebanon be cut for me. My servants will join your servants, and I will give you whatever wages you set for your servants; for you know that there is no one among us who knows how to cut timber like the Sidonians.'" (I Kings 5:1–2, 5–6).

Hiram willingly agreed to Solomon's proposal. But as a good Phoenician trader, Hiram clearly states the benefits that both kings will receive in this friendly agreement. First Book of Kings records Hiram's response:

"'I have heard the message that you have sent to me; I will fulfill all your needs in the matter of cedar and cypress timber. My servants shall bring it down to the sea from the Lebanon; I will make it into rafts to go by sea to the place you indicate. I will have them broken up there for you to take away. And you shall meet my needs by providing food for my household.'" (I Kings 5:8–9).

According to the First Book of Kings, it took Solomon seven years to build the temple (I Kings 6:37). And in payment, every year Solomon gave Hiram a certain amount of food for his services, about 240,000 bushels of wheat and 240,000 gallons of pure olive oil (I Kings 5:25).

Afterward, Solomon also wanted to build a palace, so he continued to count on Hiram for the needed materials and assistance.

"King Solomon built a fleet . . . on the shore of the Red Sea. . . . Hiram sent his servants with the fleet, sailors who were familiar with the sea, together with the servants of Solomon" (I Kings 9:26–27). "Moreover, the fleet of Hiram, which carried gold from Ophir, brought from Ophir a great quantity of almug wood and precious stones." (I Kings 10:11).   *(Continued)*

"Solomon was building his own house thirteen years" (I Kings 7:1).
"At the end of twenty years, in which Solomon had built the two houses, the
house of the Lord and the king's house, King Hiram of Tyre having supplied
Solomon with cedar and cypress timber and gold, as much as he desired, King
Solomon gave to Hiram twenty cities of the land of Galilee" (I Kings 9:10–11).

1. Why was King Hiram already friendly toward King Solomon?

Hiram had been a friend of Solomon's father, King David.

_____

2. What was the first thing King Solomon needed for the temple?

cedar and cypress timber

_____

3. How did King Hiram say he would deliver the material to King Solomon?

He would make rafts of the timber and float them on the sea to wherever Solomon wanted them.

_____

_____

4. What did Hiram receive in return for this service each year?

about 240,000 bushels of wheat and about 240,000 gallons of pure olive oil

_____

5. Why did Solomon expand his trade relationship with Hiram into the Red Sea?

Solomon needed other materials to build a palace.

_____

6. How long did it take to complete the temple and the palace?

It took seven years to complete the temple and thirteen years to complete the palace, a total

of 20 years.

_____

7. How do we know that the first agreement was changed and that food from Solomon
was no longer enough to cover Hiram's expenses on these projects?

At the end of the projects, Solomon gave Hiram 20 cities in Galilee.

_____

HOW TO FOLLOW ROUTES ON A MAP

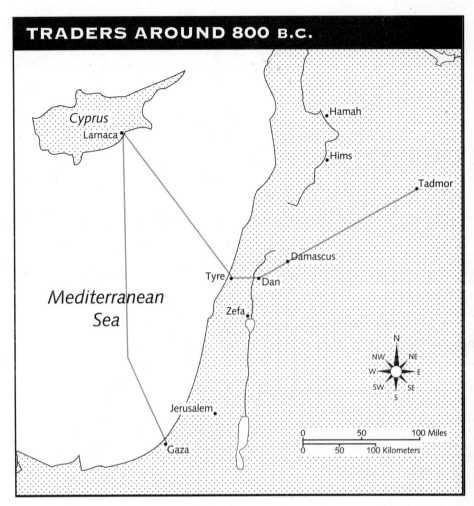

TRADERS AROUND 800 B.C.

Cyprus
Larnaca
Hamah
Hims
Tadmor
Damascus
Tyre
Dan
Mediterranean Sea
Zefa
Jerusalem
Gaza

0   50   100 Miles
0   50   100 Kilometers

You are a Lydian trader in 800 B.C., carrying spices and embroidered garments. You are on your way to meet a Phoenician ship at a seaport in western Mesopotamia.

Apply Map Skills

DIRECTIONS: Use the compass rose on the map above to chart your course. As you read the description of the trip below, fill in the names of the places you visit on the lines to the right.

You start from Tadmor. First, you travel southwest for about 130 miles. You reach (**1**), where you buy food and supplies.

You continue to travel southwest for another 30 miles, and you arrive at (**2**). Here you meet a longtime friend, another Lydian trader, who has come from the Arabian Desert. He has saddles to sell. You buy some from him.

You prepare to depart before sunrise. You head west for a distance of 25 miles. You finally reach your seaport destination, (**3**).

At the seaport your goods are put on a trading ship. The ship will sail northwest for about 150 miles. Then your goods will be sold at (**4**) on the island of (**5**). Then the ship will sail south for about 195 miles, and then southeast for about 75 miles to (**6**).

1. Damascus
2. Dan
3. Tyre
4. Larnaca
5. Cyprus
6. Gaza

Harcourt Brace School Publishers

Use after reading Chapter 2, Skill Lesson, pages 78–79.

People of the
FERTILE CRESCENT

Connect Main Ideas

DIRECTIONS: Use this organizer to show that you understand how the chapter's main ideas are connected. Complete the organizer by writing three details to support each main idea.

People of the Fertile Crescent

War and Peace in the Fertile Crescent
Early civilizations protected themselves and kept order within their societies.

1. Students may mention wars to protect farmland and water rights,

2. improved weapons, growth of empires, and Hammurabi's code.

3. _____

Civilization in Mesopotamia
The people of ancient Sumer developed new ways of doing things.

1. Students may mention such innovations as the wheel, the

2. wheeled cart, flood control using dikes, the building of ziggurats,

3. development of city-states and government, and cuneiform.

Israelites, Phoenicians, and Lydians
Cultures of the Fertile Cresent contributed to change.

1. Students may mention the Israelites' belief in one God, the written

2. alphabet of the Phoenicians, and the coined money of the Lydians.

3. _____

Use after reading Chapter 2, pages 60–81.

THE Importance of the NILE

Map Skill *Locate Places on a Map*

DIRECTIONS: *The Nile River was the heart of Egyptian civilization. It ran through the center of Egypt's land and greatly influenced the Egyptian way of life. Using information from your textbook, complete the following activities.*

1. Find and label the Mediterranean Sea.

2. Find and label the Red Sea.

3. Trace the Nile River with a blue marker.

4. Draw a triangle around the delta.

5. Color the region called Lower Egypt with a green marker.

6. Label the region called Upper Egypt.

7. Place a dot at the location of Memphis and label it.

8. Circle and label the first cataract on the Nile River.

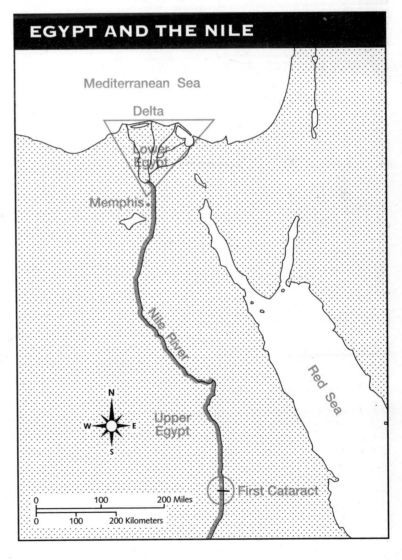

EGYPT AND THE NILE

Mediterranean Sea

Delta

Lower Egypt

Memphis

Nile River

Upper Egypt

Red Sea

First Cataract

0   100   200 Miles
0   100   200 Kilometers

Use after reading Chapter 3, Lesson 1, pages 93–97.

In Memory of
King Tutankhamen

Understand a Historical Figure

DIRECTIONS: Read the following fictional autobiography of King Tutankhamen. Then answer the questions on the following page.

As I look back now from the realm of the gods, I believe my most difficult time as pharaoh came when I was 12 years old. I'd been king for only three years when I had to make an important decision. Should I open the shrines of Osiris and the other gods that King Akhenaton had closed? Or should I follow Akhenaton's example and insist that the people forget the ancient gods and worship only the god Aton?

My vizier, Ay, told me that the priests, the army, and many other people thought that Akhenaton was a heretic who had no right to close the shrines. Ay also warned that I would bring harm to the country if I turned my back on our ancient gods. Clearly, if I did not open the shrines, I would make all of Egypt my enemy.

On the other hand, I was part of Akhenaton's family. His daughter was to be my wife. If I opened the shrines that he closed, I would make powerful enemies within the family. The priests of Aton and the court officials who had served Akhenaton would hate me.

For the good of Egypt, I knew I had to open the shrines once again. In those days, I thought that I was young and could put off giving the order to begin building my tomb. Now I see how an unpopular decision can shorten a pharaoh's reign.

But I was a god, and gods don't fear death. Yet, even gods want their deeds remembered. I am convinced that those who erase the names of past pharaohs from history are the ones who really harm Egypt. They had already begun on Akhenaton. And I was right to suspect that they would do the same to me. When Horemheb became pharaoh, he went about destroying every monument ever built in my honor. That is why I was quite happy when the stonecutters working near my tomb accidentally covered the entrance. The tomb remained sealed for 33 centuries until it was discovered in 1922 by Howard Carter.

(Continued)

Harcourt Brace School Publishers

Use after reading Chapter 3, Lesson 2, pages 98–104.

Of course, Carter's team was thrilled to find the golden death mask and thousands of carved and golden objects. But what really delighted me was their discovery of the wine jars. They had date labels that told them I ruled for ten years until my death in 1352 B.C. Finally, history would remember me for trying to do the right thing. I was also pleased when they found my fan. An inscription on its handle told them how much I enjoyed hunting in Heliopolis. Even gods have a human side. That was obvious, too, when they found that I was once a child who had fun with a toy box, a paint set, and games.

1. How long did King Tutankhamen reign, and when did he die?

He reigned for ten years and died in 1352 B.C.

2. What was the hardest decision of King Tutankhamen's life? He had to decide between

opening the shrines of Osiris and the other gods or leaving them closed as Akhenaton had done.

3. Why was this decision so difficult? He would make enemies no matter what he decided.

4. How old was King Tutankhamen when he faced that decision? He was 12 years old.

5. Using information in this autobiography, figure out how old King Tutankhamen was

when he died. He was 19 years old.

6. Why was King Tutankhamen's tomb undiscovered for 33 centuries?

The tomb's entrance had been accidentally covered by stonecutters.

7. Who discovered King Tutankhamen's tomb, and in what year? Howard Carter discovered

the tomb in 1922.

8. What artifacts helped date King Tutankhamen's reign? the wine jars

9. What artifacts give us some personal information about King Tutankhamen?

the fan with the inscription on its handle about hunting, and the toy box, paint set, and games

HOW TO SOLVE A PROBLEM

Apply Thinking Skills

DIRECTIONS: Look at the inventor's thought list below and the five steps in problem solving. Put the inventor's thoughts in order by writing the letter of each one next to the correct step in the problem-solving process.

The invention of the shadoof helped solve one major problem for early Egyptian farmers. They needed to get water from irrigation canals that were lower than the fields.

Shadoof Inventor's Thought List

a. I could pull up buckets of water with the rope. Perhaps I could tie the bucket to a pole and lift the bucket out of the water. Or I could use the pole as a lever to lift the bucket out of the canal.

b. I gathered buckets, rope, and wooden poles. I took a sturdy pole with a bucket tied to one end and a stone weight on the other. I built a crossbar to support the pole. Now I can lift the bucket and swing it over to water my field.

c. I built my invention and tried it. It works perfectly.

d. It is easier to use a lever with a bucket tied to the end than to drag buckets up with a rope. To make the lifting even easier, I could use a heavy rock to weight the other end of the pole.

e. How do I get water into my field during a drought? The water in the irrigation canal is lower than my field.

FIVE-STEP PROBLEM SOLVING

e
_____ **1.** Identify the Problem

a
_____ **2.** Think of Possible Solutions to the Problem

d
_____ **3.** Compare the Solutions, and Figure Out Which Would Work Best

b
_____ **4.** Plan How to Carry Out the Solution

c
_____ **5.** Solve the Problem, and Think About How Well the Solution Worked

Use after reading Chapter 3, Skill Lesson, page 105.

At her coronation Hatshepsut wore more than fancy clothes and jewelry. The things she wore symbolized what the pharaoh's authority meant to Egypt. No one who saw the new pharaoh doubted that she would rule with the power of the gods of Egypt.

THE PHARAOH QUEEN

Classify Information

DIRECTIONS: Read the list of things that a pharaoh symbolized to the people of Egypt. Look at the drawing of Hatshepsut. Decide what each item she is wearing symbolizes. Write the symbol's number on the blank line next to each item's description.

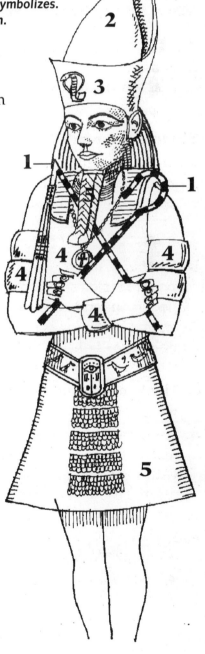

Symbols of Pharaoh's Authority and Power

1. Symbol of Osiris's immortality represented by the pharaoh

2. Symbol of political unity between Upper and Lower Egypt

3. Symbol of the gods' protection of the pharaoh

4. Symbol of Egypt's wealth and power

5. Symbol of the pharaoh's masculine strength

Queen Hatshepsut and Her Adornments

__2__ Double crown, representing Upper Egypt and Lower Egypt

__3__ Sacred cobra, on the front of the crown, that spits poisonous fire at anyone coming too near the pharaoh

__5__ Royal braided beard

__1__ Two scepters, emblems of Osiris: the golden crook and the golden flail

__4__ Gold-and-jeweled pendant

__4__ Gold bracelets and rings

__5__ Short kilt of a king

Conflict Between EGYPT *and* KUSH

Kingdoms rise and fall based on three major factors: successful leadership, military power, and ability to trade. In the long history of neighboring countries Egypt and Kush, there were periods of conflict and times of cooperation.

Interpret Data

DIRECTIONS: Look at the chart on the following page. Make a color key for Egypt and Kush by coloring in the Egypt box with one color and the Kush/Nubia box with another color. Then read about how Egypt and Kush changed. At each point, decide if the countries were strong, weak, or neutral. Use the colors to fill in the arrows. Then answer the questions below.

1. At which point were both Egypt and Kush strong? Why? In 1500 B.C. both had a center of

power, and they were partners in trade.

_____

2. When were both Egypt and Kush weak? What was happening?

In 670 B.C. Kush was forced to give up Egypt, which it controlled, to invaders from the Fertile

Crescent. In 350 B.C. Kush was defeated by Axum.

_____

3. Kush twice bounced back from defeat by invaders. When and how? In 1500 B.C. and

again in 650 B.C., Kushite leaders moved their capital and reopened trade routes.

_____

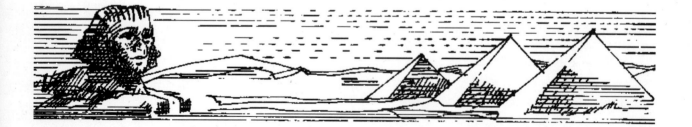

(Continued)

Use after reading Chapter 3, Lesson 4, pages 111–115.

Harcourt Brace School Publishers

KEY

▨ Egypt   ▒ Kush/Nubia

WEAK	NEUTRAL	STRONG

Egypt takes over and divides Nubia.

2000 B.C.

Hyksos conquer Egypt. Kush becomes free-trade center.

1670 B.C.

Egypt drives out Hyksos and regains Nubia.

1521 B.C.

WEAK	NEUTRAL	STRONG

Egypt in power. Kush moves to Napata, trades with Egypt.

1500 B.C.

Egypt's leadership begins to weaken.

1365 B.C.

Kush defeats Egypt.

750 B.C.

WEAK	NEUTRAL	STRONG

Kush loses control of Egypt to invaders from Fertile Crescent.

670 B.C.

Kush rebuilds strength by moving capital and trade to Meroë.

650 B.C.

Kush no longer on trade route. Kush defeated by Axum.

350 B.C.

Harcourt Brace School Publishers

AFRICAN CIVILIZATIONS
of the Nile Valley

Connect Main Ideas

DIRECTIONS: *Use this organizer to show that you understand how the chapter's main ideas are connected. Complete the organizer by writing three details to support each main idea.*

The Importance of the Nile River
The physical setting of the Nile Valley affected the development of civilization in North Africa.

1. The Nile provided water for drinking and farming and deposited fertile soil

2. in its delta. Also, warm, sunny weather allowed for two or three harvests

3. each year.

African Civilizations of the Nile Valley

The Dynasties of Egypt
The ancient Egyptian people maintained their civilization for centuries while making some changes.

1. Egypt stayed the same
by maintaining one
religion for a long time
2. and by being ruled by
long-standing
dynasties. Changes
3. included growth of the
middle class and
conquest of Nubia.

Kush: Egypt's Rival
The people of Nubia and the people of Egypt influenced each other.

1. Empire-building
pharaohs invaded
Nubia; Kush's armies
2. took over Egypt;
merchants exchanged
goods; Egypt built
3. trading centers in Nubia.

Harcourt Brace School Publishers

Use after reading Chapter 3, pages 92–119.

Life in the City

    Archaeologists first excavated the Harappan cities of the Indus Valley in the 1920s and 1930s. Walled cities, about three miles (5 kilometers) in diameter, contained government buildings, a huge grain shed on a raised upper level, and wide streets laid out in squares. Life in Harappan cities was well advanced for its time.

Make Observations

DIRECTIONS: This drawing shows how a house in a Harappan city may have looked. Study the picture. Recall what you have read in your text about Harappan architecture. Then answer the questions below.

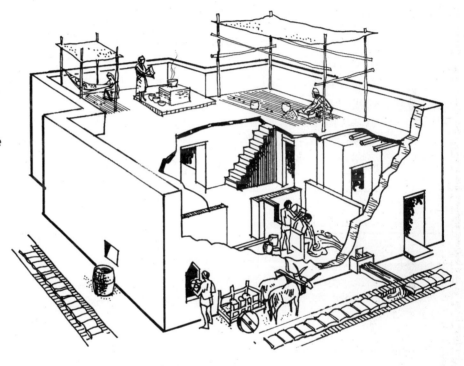

1. What "modern" conveniences do you see? <u>drains for water from bathroom, covered sewers</u>

<u>in the street, chute for garbage</u>

2. Thick brick walls without windows helped keep the house cool. Why do you think

the house was built on an open courtyard? <u>for natural light and fresh air</u>

_____

3. What other means of staying cool do you see? <u>bathing, awnings on the roof for shade,</u>

<u>cooking on the roof</u>

In the Beginning

Use Source Material

DIRECTIONS: Read the Chinese myth that tells about the creation of the world. Then answer the questions that follow.

In the beginning the world was an enormous egg. Outside the egg was only darkness. Inside was only chaos—and a sleeping giant named Pan Gu. After a long time, Pan Gu woke up and cracked out of the eggshell. Part of the egg escaped and floated up to form the sky. The heavier part of the egg sank down and became the Earth. Pan Gu was worried that they might go back together, so he stood holding the Earth down with his giant feet and pushing the sky up with his arms. He kept the Earth and sky apart for thousands of years. Then Pan Gu lay down to die. Every part of Pan Gu was used to make the universe. His breath was turned into wind and clouds, and his voice into thunder. His left eye became the sun, his right eye became the moon, and his hair became the stars in the sky. His arms and legs grew into mountains, and his veins were roads and paths. Pan Gu's flesh turned into the soil in the fields, and his skin was the plants and trees. His bones and teeth were minerals buried in the earth, and his sweat became dew and rain. The fleas on the body of the giant Pan Gu evolved into the first people.

1. According to Chinese mythology, what did Pan Gu give the Chinese people?

He gave them everything they needed to live in the universe.

_____

2. Does the story of Pan Gu help you understand why the Chinese people believed

their world was the center of the universe? Explain. Yes; it tells how the whole universe

was created around them.

3. Do you think the story makes individuals seem important or unimportant? Explain.

It makes people seem unimportant, like fleas. Nature is bigger and more important.

_____

4. How did the Chinese people think of their gods? as very powerful

_____

Use after reading Chapter 4, Lesson 2, pages 126–131.

Harcourt Brace School Publishers

HOW TO USE AN Elevation Map

The Harappan civilization stretched for at least 500 miles (800 km) along the Indus River. A sheltered valley and lower elevation meant warmer temperatures for people as well as for crops. Today the Indus valley still holds numerous cities and towns.

Apply Map Skills

DIRECTIONS: The elevation map below shows a portion of modern-day Pakistan and its surroundings. Study the map and the elevation key, and then answer the questions.

ELEVATION MAP OF INDUS VALLEY AREA

Feet	Meters
Above 13,120	Above 4,000
6,560	2,000
1,640	500
655	200
0	0
Below sea level	

0   100   200 Miles
0   100 200 Kilometers
Two-Point Equidistant Projection

Harcourt Brace School Publishers

(Continued)

Use after reading Chapter 4, Skills Lesson, pages 132–133.

1. Find the city of Larkana. In what elevation range does it lie?
   0–655 feet

2. If you traveled from Sahiwal to Larkana, would you be higher, lower, or at the
   same elevation? You would be at the same elevation.

3. Find the city of Bikaner. In what elevation range does it lie?
   655–1,640 feet

4. Sahiwal lies in an elevation range that is different from that of Bikaner. What is the
   elevation of the line that separates these two ranges? 655 feet

5. What is that line called? a contour line

6. If you traveled 600 miles (966 km) northeast from Sahiwal to Dharmsala, would you
   need warmer or cooler clothing? Why? warmer clothing, because Dharmsala is at a much
   higher elevation

7. Why do you think the Harappan people traded with Sumer instead of China?
   It was too difficult to establish a trade route across high elevations to trade with China.

8. Why do you think Harappan traders sailed by way of the Arabian Sea to trade
   with Sumer instead of taking an overland route? The high elevations west of the Indus River
   were too difficult to cross.

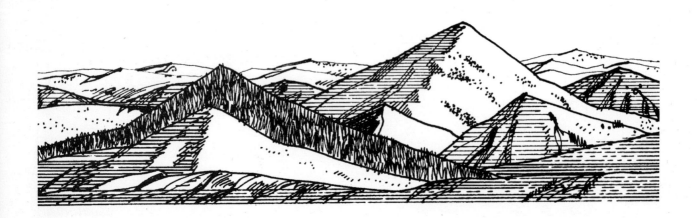

Use after reading Chapter 4, Skill Lesson, pages 132–133.

WHO Did It?

You have learned about six different cultures. They were alike in some important ways, but they also had significant differences.

Classify Information

DIRECTIONS: *Match the six early cultures listed below with the phrases that describe them. Write the first initial—for example, C for Chinese—in the blank. The number at the end of each description tells you how many cultures fit the description.*

C CHINESE	E EGYPTIAN	H HARAPPAN	K KUSHITE	M MAYAN	O OLMEC

CEHKMO _____ based economy on farming (6)

EMO _____ developed calendar (3)

EKM _____ built pyramids (3)

E _____ believed ruler was a god (1)

C _____ used pictograph writing (1)

H _____ built carefully planned cities (1)

MO _____ worshipped jaguar rain god (2)

CEHK _____ traded with other peoples (4)

M _____ used a number system with a symbol for zero (1)

E _____ wrote on papyrus (1)

H _____ used standard weights and measures (1)

K _____ invented alphabet of 23 letters (1)

H _____ built cities on mounds to avoid flooding (1)

C _____ believed they were center of the universe (1)

CEK _____ believed in life after death (3)

H _____ baked bricks in ovens (1)

EKMO _____ used hieroglyphic writing (4)

CEHKMO _____ lived near rivers that flooded (6)

K _____ produced iron (1)

C _____ raised silkworms for silk cloth (1)

CEKMO _____ built temples (5)

O _____ carved huge stone faces (1)

HOW TO LEARN FROM ARTIFACTS

Apply Visual Thinking Skills

Directions: Below are drawings of artifacts from three different civilizations and three different parts of the world. Study the drawings and read the descriptions. Draw a line from each drawing to the description that correctly identifies it. Then answer the questions below.

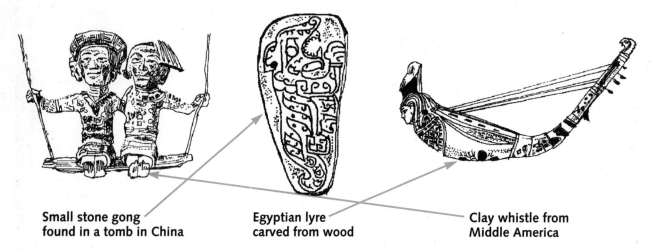

Small stone gong found in a tomb in China

Egyptian lyre carved from wood

Clay whistle from Middle America

1. What is the common purpose of the three artifacts shown above?

They are all musical instruments,

_____

_____

2. What do these artifacts tell you about the people who lived 3,500 years ago?

They had the time and ability to create music and art.

_____

_____

_____

Use after reading Chapter 4, Skill Lesson, pages 138–139.

Harcourt Brace School Publishers

Early Civilizations in Asia and the Americas

Connect Main Ideas

DIRECTIONS: Use this organizer to show you understand how the chapter's main ideas are connected. Complete the organizer by writing three details to support each main idea.

Civilization in the Indus Valley
The physical setting of the Indus Valley civilization affected its development and survival.

1. The Indus and four tributaries bring water to the valley. The flooding rivers deposit fertile silt on the plain. The rivers also

2. deposit stones, which people piled up to build villages that were safe from floods.

3.

Civilization in the Huang He Valley
The beliefs of the ancient Chinese people affected the development and growth of their civilization.

1. Possible responses: the Chinese believed they were at the center of the universe,

2. their rulers had a mandate from heaven, oracles developed and early writing

3. system, and people who could write ran the government and controlled society.

Early Civilizations in Asia and the Americas

Ancient Civilizations of the Americas
The Mayas both built on the achievements of the Olmec civilization and contributed their own.

1. The Mayas built cities and cleared land for farming.

2. Religion was important, the jaguar was a rain god.

3. The Mayas developed a 365-day calendar and a numbering system using the zero.

Confucius Said...

The followers of Confucius wrote down his teachings in the form of proverbs, or short sayings. His teachings became a guide for the way many people lived. The following sayings are based on the *Analects of Confucius*.

Understand Ideas and Values

DIRECTIONS: Read the sayings of Confucius below. Then look at the sentences on page 31. Write whether Confucius would have agreed or disagreed with each statement. Explain your answer.

SOME SAYINGS OF CONFUCIUS

- Good people bring out what is good in others, not what is bad.

- To eat your fill but not apply your mind to anything all day is a problem. Are there no games to play? Even that would be smarter than doing nothing.

- People who do not think far enough ahead always have worries near at hand.

- Don't worry that no one recognizes you; seek to be worthy of recognition.

- Speak truthfully and guide your friends in good ways. If they do not agree, then stop and do not follow them.

- When everyone dislikes something, it should be examined. When everyone likes something, it should be examined.

- If you make a mistake and do not correct it, this is the real mistake.

(Continued)

1. It is all right for children to watch television all day during summer vacation.

Confucius would disagree. They should look for something useful to do. They could read, study, or at least play a game.

2. You have an influence on your friends. Confucius would agree. You should set a good example and try to help your friends do what is right.

3. Follow the crowd. Confucius would disagree. You should examine, or look carefully at, what "everyone" likes or dislikes and then make your own decision.

4. Don't bother to plan ahead, because your plans usually will not work out.

Confucius would disagree. If you don't make plans, you'll worry about what will happen.

5. Learn from your mistakes. Confucius would agree. The real mistake is in failing to improve.

6. Be sure that everyone knows who you are. Confucius would disagree. It is more important to be worthy of recognition than to have it.

Use after reading Chapter 5, Lesson 1, pages 155–159.

HOW TO IDENTIFY CAUSES and their EFFECTS

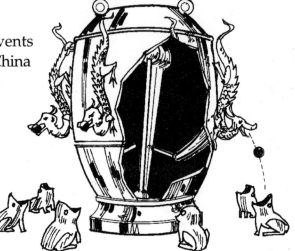

As you have seen before in history, natural events have led to important inventions. Earthquakes in China have been recorded since 780 B.C. During the Han dynasty, Chang Heng invented a seismograph, a device for detecting earthquakes.

Apply Thinking Skills

DIRECTIONS: Look at the drawing of Chang Heng's seismograph, and read the description. Then read each pair of statements below. Decide which is the cause and which is the effect. Indicate each by marking the statements with C (Cause) or E (Effect).

The seismograph was a beautifully decorated bronze jar. Inside was a pendulum (a weight hung so that it could swing back and forth) and eight bronze levers. When an earthquake occurred in China, it caused the pendulum to strike one of the levers. The lever in turn opened a dragon's jaws. When it did so, the bronze ball the dragon was holding in its mouth fell into the open mouth of the frog squatting below it. As a result, Chang Heng knew that an earthquake had taken place. He also knew where it had happened, because the path of the bronze ball indicated from which direction the tremor had come.

1. _____E_____ Chang Heng invented a device to detect earthquakes.

_____C_____ Earthquakes shook ancient China.

2. _____E_____ A pendulum inside the jar struck a lever.

_____C_____ An earthquake occurred.

3. _____C_____ A bronze lever in the seismograph was struck.

_____E_____ A dragon on the outside of the jar opened its jaw.

4. _____E_____ The ball fell into a frog's mouth.

_____C_____ A dragon opened its jaw.

5. _____C_____ Chang Heng found a ball in a frog's mouth.

_____E_____ Chang Heng knew from which direction the tremor had come.

Use after reading Chapter 5, Skill Lesson, page 160.

Read MORE About It

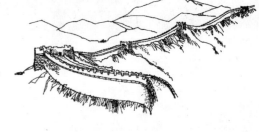

Learn More About a Subject

DIRECTIONS: The Great Wall of China has been called one of the great wonders of the world. Read more about it below. Use this information and your textbook as background to answer the questions that follow.

Did you know that the only human-made structure on the surface of the Earth that can be seen from space is the Great Wall of China? Some parts of the wall were built by the rulers of small rival kingdoms as long ago as the fifth century B.C. These rulers wished to protect their territories from one another and from barbarians who sometimes attacked from the north. In the third century B.C., the emperor Shi Huangdi crushed the power of the nobles and built a strong empire. He ordered that the northern walls be united into a single line of defense. All available material was used: clay, stone, willow branches, reeds, and sand. When completed, the wall was so wide that five horses or ten soldiers on foot could travel side by side on its top. In times of danger a fire was built atop a watchtower. The smoke would alert soldiers in the next tower. During the Ming dynasty (A.D. 1368–1644), the wall was repaired and parts of it were rebuilt. In many places brick and stone slabs replaced the clay and earth. The Great Wall again became the symbol of a strong empire.

1. How is the Great Wall a symbol of Shi Huangdi's great empire?

He joined parts of smaller walls into one great wall, just as he unified small rival kingdoms into

one great empire.

2. How does the building of the Great Wall illustrate Shi Huangdi's style of governing?

He was a cruel and demanding ruler. He used the peasants to build the wall, and thousands of

them died.

3. Why was the Great Wall built only along the northern border of China?

Invaders came from the north; China had natural barriers of ocean, desert, and mountains on the

other sides.

4. Why do you think the wall was built so wide?   to allow the army to move quickly to

wherever they were needed

THE HAN HERITAGE

The period of the Han dynasty was a time of peace, wealth, and progress. It is sometimes called the Golden Age of China because many branches of arts and learning blossomed.

Organize Information

DIRECTIONS: *Each oval in the web below tells about an invention or advance made during the Han dynasty. Match each invention or advance with the area or field of knowledge shown in the box. Then write the term on the appropriate line in the web.*

government	language	trade	history	philosophy	technology

Confucianism became official teaching; Daoism was also supported.

philosophy

Ambassadors were sent to make peace; civil service was established.

government

Wheelbarrow was developed.

technology

The Silk Road was opened.

trade

Paper was invented; first Chinese dictionary was written.

language

Sima Qian recorded China's past.

history

Use after reading Chapter 5, Lesson 3, pages 166–170.

HOW TO CLASSIFY INFORMATION

Apply Thinking Skills

DIRECTIONS: Review the list of words below. Then place the words into five different groups, or classifications. Write an appropriate heading for each classification.

Africa	Daoism	ivory	silk
apricots	Europe	Legalism	Sima Qian
Central Asia	gold	Mediterranean Sea	wool
Chang'an	Han dynasty	Qin dynasty	Zhou dynasty
China	Gao Zu	Shang dynasty	
Confucianism	iron	Shi Huangdi	

Periods or Empires

Han dynasty

Qin dynasty

Shang dynasty

Zhou dynasty

People

Gao Zu

Shi Huangdi

Sima Qian

Philosophies

Confucianism

Daoism

Legalism

Places

Africa

Central Asia

Chang'an

China

Europe

Mediterranean Sea

Goods or Trade Items

apricots

gold

iron

ivory

silk

wool

Use after reading Chapter 5, Skill Lesson, page 171.

CHINA

Connect Main Ideas

DIRECTIONS: Use this organizer to show that you understand how the chapter's main ideas are connected. Complete the organizer by writing a sentence or two describing each topic.

China

Progress Under the Han Dynasty

Under the Han, China experienced a Golden Age. Language, history, philosophy, and religion blossomed. Paper, the wheelbarrow, and the seismograph were just some of the inventions of the Han period.

_____

United Rule in the Qin Dynasty

The Harsh ruler of the Qin, Shi Huangdi, united China beginning around 221 B.C. Shi Huangdi forced peasants to work on the Great Wall and brought standardization to China.

_____

_____

The Zhou Dynasty

The Zhou used iron weapons to defeat the Shang. In 1122 B.C., they claimed the Mandate of Heaven. The Zhou created a new social structure to rule its large kingdom.

_____

_____

1122 B.C. to A.D. 230

Harcourt Brace School Publishers

Use after reading Chapter 5, pages 155–173.

A Family of Languages

Almost half the people in the world today speak an Indo-European language. English is an Indo-European language. So is Hindi, which is spoken by many people in India. Hindi is one of the modern languages that came from Sanskrit, the ancient language that one group of Indo-Europeans, the Aryans, brought to India.

Find Similarities

DIRECTIONS: *The table below has a column for each of five languages. The first four columns show some common words in Sanskrit, Greek, Latin and German. These four languages, as well as English, are from the Indo-European family of languages. See how the words are alike. In each space in the English column write the English word that you think fits. The words in the box below may help you.*

brother	mother	sister
daughter	new	three
father	seven	

SANSKRIT	GREEK	LATIN	GERMAN	ENGLISH
matar	meter	mater	mutter	mother
pitar	pater	pater	vater	father
bhratar	adelphos	frater	bruder	brother
svasar	adelphe	soror	schwester	sister
duhitar	thugater	filia	tochter	daughter
navos	neos	novus	neu	new
trayas	treis	tres	drei	three
sapta	hepta	septem	seiben	seven

HOW TO USE A CULTURAL MAP

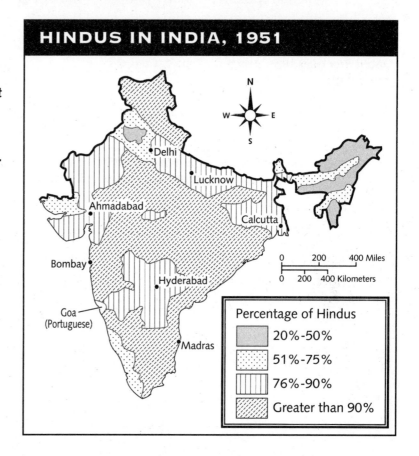

HINDUS IN INDIA, 1951

Apply Thinking Skills

DIRECTIONS: The map on page 181 of your textbook shows languages and religions of the Indian subcontinent today. Hinduism is the most popular religion in India. The map at the right shows the distribution of Hindus in India shortly after India's independence. Use this map to answer the questions below.

Percentage of Hindus

- 20%-50%
- 51%-75%
- 76%-90%
- Greater than 90%

1. Which region of India had the lowest percentage of Hindus? the northeast _____

2. What percentage of the population was Hindu in the area surrounding Madras?

greater than 90% _____

3. In 1951 what was the name of the Portuguese possession on the west coast of India?

Goa _____

4. What percentage of the population was Hindu in the area to the east of Goa?

76%–90% _____

5. Did any parts of India have a population of less than 20% Hindu? How can you tell?

no, because the lowest entry in the key begins with 20% _____

Use after reading Chapter 6, Skill Lesson, pages 180–181.

Harcourt Brace School Publishers

NAME _____ DATE _____

An American Folktale

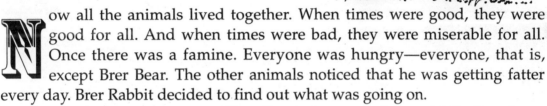

Like many peoples around the globe, Americans tell folktales. Some were told by enslaved Africans who were brought to America.

Learn from Literature

DIRECTIONS: Read the following American folktale about Brer (meaning "Brother") Rabbit. Then answer the questions that follow.

Brer Rabbit, Brer Bear, and the Honey

Now all the animals lived together. When times were good, they were good for all. And when times were bad, they were miserable for all. Once there was a famine. Everyone was hungry—everyone, that is, except Brer Bear. The other animals noticed that he was getting fatter every day. Brer Rabbit decided to find out what was going on.

One night he went over to Brer Bear's house and found Miz Bear busy putting ashes from the fireplace into a big bag. "What in the world are you doing?" he asked her. "Brer Bear asked me to fix him up a big bag of ashes every evening," she replied. "I don't know what he does with 'em!"

Brer Rabbit said good night to Miz Bear, and he went out and hid behind a tree. After he was sure Miz Bear was asleep, he sneaked back into the house and poked a little hole in the bag of ashes. At dawn the next morning, he watched Brer Bear leave the house with the bag over his shoulder. At a safe distance, Brer Rabbit followed the trail of ashes Brer Bear left behind. He followed him into the woods, over hills, and through a briar patch.

At the end of the trail, he found Brer Bear. He was sitting high in a poplar tree eating honey. What a sight he was! He had poured the ashes all over himself to keep the bees from stinging him.

Then Brer Rabbit saw that all the trees around were dripping with honey. His stomach started growling like crazy. He rushed back to tell all the other animals why Brer Bear was getting so fat. "And I know how we can get some of that honey," he added.

Brer Rabbit led the animals right to the edge of the grove of honey trees. He told the big animals to stand behind the trees and bushes. "When I holler, shake these trees and bushes as hard as you can," he instructed. He sent the insects up into the trees and said, "When I holler, beat your wings as hard as you can." He hid the little animals in the tall grass. "When I holler, run through the grass as hard as you can," he told them.

(Continued)

Harcourt Brace School Publishers

Then Brer Rabbit took a long rope and went into the honey grove. "Brer Bear," he called. "There's a hurricane coming! I'm getting ready to tie myself to a tree so I don't get blown away." Then he hollered, "CAN YOU HEAR IT COMING, BRER BEAR?" Then all the animals started shaking the trees and bushes, beating their wings in the air, and rushing through the tall grass. Brer Bear hurried down from the tree, begging, "Tie me to the tree with you, Brer Rabbit."

Brer Rabbit quickly tied Brer Bear to the tree, and when he pulled the last knot tight, he hollered again, "COME AND SEE BRER BEAR!"

All the animals came and laughed at Brer Bear. Then they filled their stomachs with honey and took a lot more home for the next day.

1. Many folktales use animal characters. Why do you think that is so?

In a story, animals can talk and act like humans. They can be used to get the message across

without making the story seem too serious.

2. Do you see a similarity between this story and the *Jataka Tales*?

Both have morals, or lessons, for the listener.

3. What message do you think the enslaved Africans may have heard in this tale?

It's not right for one, or a few, to have more than others. Those who have less may find a way to

make things equal.

4. Why does this story still appeal to us today? We like the way Brer Rabbit tricks the greedy

Brer Bear. We like to see "the little guy" win.

Harcourt Brace School Publishers

NAME _____ DATE _____

The Influence of Asoka

Draw Conclusions

DIRECTIONS: Read the paragraphs on this page. Use this information and your textbook to answer the questions below.

India

Sri Lanka

The Wheel of Asoka is shown on the flag of India. This wheel design was carved on the stone pillars that proclaimed the edicts of the emperor Asoka. The Wheel of Asoka represents law.

To spread his law, Asoka sent his son Mahendra to lead a group of Buddhist missionaries to the nearby island of Ceylon (present-day Sri Lanka). The king of Ceylon, his court, and most of the people converted to Buddhism. Sri Lanka is still mostly Buddhist.

1. The wheel and the lion, two designs used by Asoka, are symbols of modern India.

Why do you think Asoka is honored in India today? Asoka is remembered and honored

because he used his authority to better the lives of his people.

_____

2. Would you say that Mahendra was more like his father, Asoka, or his

great-grandfather, Chandragupta? Explain your answer. Mahendra was more like Asoka,

who lived according to the peaceful ways of Buddhism. Chandragupta was cruel and brutal.

_____

3. In what way did the island kingdom of Ceylon follow Asoka more closely than did

Asoka's own country of India? After Asoka's death many of his ideas were forgotten and

Buddhism faded away in India. Buddhism has continued to flourish in Sri Lanka.

_____

4. Based on what you have learned about the Maurya Empire in India, what are two ways a ruler can unite the people of a country? Which do you think is the better way?

Explain your answer. A ruler can unite people by force or by fairness. Accept answers that the

students can support.

_____

Harcourt Brace School Publishers

Superior
MILITARY
Technology

Make Comparisons

DIRECTIONS: Read the two "news reports" below. Then look at the military technology listed in the box on the next page. Write the name of each item in the correct column, according to the army that used it.

CYRUS CONQUERS PERSIA

PERSIA—Cyrus the Great has overpowered kingdoms from the Indus River to beyond the Nile. A smart strategist, Cyrus knows how to use the great number of soldiers at his command. His conquest of Babylon has freed the Jews held captive there, and he has allowed them to return to their own land. Their prophet Isaiah has written that Cyrus "tramples kings under foot; he makes them like dust with his sword, like driven stubble with his bow". The historian Herodotus credits Cyrus's success to his growing up in a tribe of tough herdsmen and horsemen. "Soft countries breed soft men," he commented. Cyrus and his followers "chose to live in a rugged land and rule rather than to cultivate rich plains and be slaves."

UN FORCES WIN IN GULF

PERSIAN GULF—Just before dawn on August 2, 1990, Iraq took control of the much smaller country of Kuwait. The U.S. and 27 other countries condemned the invasion and demanded that Iraq withdraw. Saddam Hussein, president of Iraq, refused. Most other nations cut off trade with Iraq. Hussein declared that Kuwait was now part of Iraq. In November the U.S. powered up for war by sending troops, tanks, aircraft, and ships to the Persian Gulf area. The United Nations Security Council gave Iraq a deadline for withdrawal. Negotiations continued. On January 17, 1991, U.S. and allied forces fought back. Their high-tech weaponry stunned Iraq. On February 27 Kuwait was liberated, and a cease-fire was declared.

Harcourt Brace School Publishers

(Continued)

Use after reading Chapter 6, Lesson 4, pages 192–195.

NAME _____ DATE _____

SUPERIOR MILITARY TECHNOLOGY OF THE TIME

Patriot missiles

War chariot wheels with sharp knives

Stealth fighter jets

Apache helicopters

Soldiers riding horses and camels

Bronze helmets and shields

Night-vision goggles

Tomahawk cruise missiles

CYRUS THE GREAT'S ARMY	UNITED NATIONS FORCES
War chariot wheels with sharp knives	Patriot missiles
Soldiers riding horses and camels	Stealth fighter jets
Bronze helmets and shields	Apache helicopters
	Night-vision goggles
	Tomahawk cruise missiles

Harcourt Brace School Publishers

INDIA & PERSIA

Connect Main Ideas

DIRECTIONS: Use this organizer to show that you understand how the chapter's main ideas are connected. Complete the organizer by writing two details to support each main idea.

India and Persia

Aryans Bring Changes to India
The arrival of the Aryans changed life for the early people of India.

1. Students may mention that the natives of India had to compete with the Aryans for farmland, that the Aryans

2. brought a new language and religion to India, and that the Aryans began the caste system.

United Rule in India
Maurya and Gupta rulers used different methods to unite India.

1. Students may mention Chandragupta's harsh rule and contrast it with Asoka's more fair rule.

2. _____

The Persian Empire
Strong leaders played an important role in the development of the Persian Empire and its civilization.

1. Students may mention the roles of Cyrus as an empire builder, Darius as an organizer of a large empire, and

2. Zarathustra as the messenger of religious ideas.

Harcourt Brace School Publishers

Use after reading Chapter 6, pages 174–197.

NAME _____ DATE _____

A Nation of *Islands, Peninsulas, & Water*

🌐 *Locate Features on a Map*

DIRECTIONS: Greece is a nation of islands and peninsulas. Use your textbook and the map below to complete the following activities.

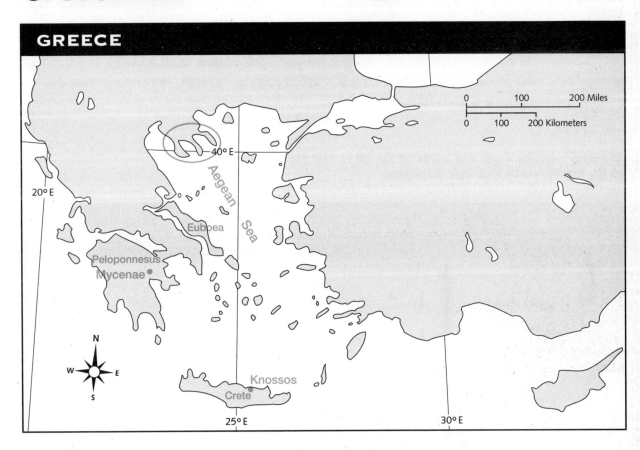

GREECE

1. Label the Aegean Sea, which separates Greece from Turkey.

2. Find and label Crete, Greece's largest island.

3. Euboea, Greece's second-largest island, is located along the western side of the Aegean Sea. Label it.

4. Find and label Greece's largest peninsula, the Peloponnesus.

5. Circle the three peninsulas located in the northwest part of the Aegean Sea.

6. Place a dot at the location of Knossos and label it.

7. Place a second dot at the location of Mycenae and label it.

Use after reading Chapter 7, Lesson 1, pages 211–215.

Using Greek Root Words

English is a combination of many languages. It contains words that come from French, German, Latin, and Greek. Many English words are a combination of shorter words from these languages. These are called **root words.** Just as the roots of a tree form its base, root words form the base for many English words.

Greek root words are often used as prefixes (beginnings of words) and suffixes (endings of words). Examples of words that include Greek prefixes and suffixes are **democracy** and **telephone.** Democracy is made up of two Greek words. The prefix *demos* means "people," and the suffix *cracy* means "rule." If you put the two parts together, you can figure out that *democracy* means "rule by the people." *Tele* comes from a Greek word meaning "far," and *phone* comes from a Greek word meaning "sound." Knowing this, do you think the telephone is well-named?

Use Word Origins

DIRECTIONS: Use the Greek root words on the left to help you match the English words with their definitions.

GREEK ROOT WORDS	ENGLISH WORDS	DEFINITIONS
anti = against or opposite	1. __h__ antibiotic	a. a five-sided figure
athlon = athlete	2. __f__ bibliography	b. telling about a subject through pictures
biblio = book	3. __d__ chronometer	c. a secret written message
bios = life	4. __c__ cryptograph	d. an instrument for measuring time
chronos = time	5. __i__ decathlon	e. the study of life
crypt = secret or hidden	6. __j__ geology	f. a list of books
deca = ten	7. __b__ iconography	g. an instrument used to measure heat
geo = earth	8. __e__ biology	h. a chemical that destroys microorganisms
gon = having many angles	9. __a__ pentagon	i. a ten-event athletic contest
graphy = writing	10. __g__ thermometer	j. the study of the Earth
icon = image		
logy = study of		
meter = measure		
penta = five		
thermos = heat		

Use after reading Chapter 7, Lesson 2, pages 216–221.

Harcourt Brace School Publishers

HERODOTUS
AND THE PERSIAN WARS

In *The Persian Wars*, Herodotus wrote about many battles, but most of this book describes regional customs and geography. As a result, he is considered to be not only the world's first historian, but also its first geographer. He recorded his observations from his many travels, and although it is not always accurate, he wrote an entertaining narrative.

Use Source Material

**DIRECTIONS: Read each of the following quotations from
The Persian Wars. Then answer the questions that follow.**

"[The Babylonians] have no physicians, but when a man is ill, they lay him in the public square, and the passers-by come up to him, and if they have ever had his disease themselves, or have known anyone who has suffered from it, they give him advice, recommending him to do whatever they found good in their own case, or in the case known to them. And no one is allowed to pass the sick man in silence without asking him what his ailment is."

1. What do you think might have been the strengths and weaknesses of such a system?

Accept answers that have a logical explanation based on student experiences. Strengths may

include that people who have had experience with a disease are likely to know a lot about it.

Weaknesses may include that such people may not have known how they, or their friends,

were cured.

_____

_____

2. Would this system work today? Explain your answer. probably not; because the passers-

by could catch communicable diseases, and because doctors could cure more people

_____

_____

_____

(Continued)

"Assyria possesses a vast number of great cities, whereof the most renowned and strongest at this time was Babylon. . . . The following is a description of the place: The city stands on a broad plain, and is an exact square, fifteen miles in length each way. . . . In magnificence there is no other city that approaches to it. It is surrounded . . . by a broad and deep moat, full of water, behind which rises a wall [335 feet wide and 85 feet high].

"And here I may not omit to tell the use to which the mould dug out of the great moat was turned, nor the manner wherein the wall was wrought [constructed]. As fast as they dug the moat the soil which they got from the cutting was made into bricks, and when a sufficient number were completed they baked the bricks in kilns. Then they set to building, and began with bricking the borders of the moat, after which they proceeded to construct the wall itself, using throughout for their cement hot bitumen [asphalt], and interposing a layer of . . . reeds at every thirtieth course of the bricks. On the top, along the edges of the wall, they constructed buildings. . . . In the circuit of the wall are 100 gates, all of brass. . . . The bitumen used in the work was brought to Babylon from the Is, a small stream which flows into the Euphrates at the point where the city of the same name stands eight days' journey from Babylon."

1. What is a moat? a body of water surrounding a fortification

_____

_____

2. What do you think was the purpose of the moat? protection

_____

_____

3. Do you think the Assyrians made good use of their local resources? Explain

your answer. yes; because they used local mud to make bricks, straw to strengthen walls,

bitumen as a cement, and they built their city on the plain between the rivers.

_____

_____

_____

_____

_____

Use after reading Chapter 7, Lesson 3, pages 222–227.

Harcourt Brace School Publishers

HOW TO PREDICT LIKELY OUTCOMES

Apply Thinking Skills

DIRECTIONS: In the table below are five events that took place in ancient Greece. Below the table is a list of possible outcomes for these events. Write the letter of the appropriate outcomes on the line at the right of each event. You may use some outcomes more than once.

EVENT	POSSIBLE OUTCOMES
Volcanic activity on Crete	b, g
Development of Minoan trade	a, e, h
Development of city-states	c, d, f
Greek victory in Persian Wars	b, e, i
Olympic Games	i

a. sharing of customs

b. destruction of property

c. rise of various forms of government

d. establishment of colonies

e. extension of Greek culture

f. development of political rivalries

g. destruction of historical records

h. spread of technology, language, and religion

i. development of Greek unity

Use after reading Chapter 7, Skill Lesson, page 228.

ALEXANDER THE GREAT
Learns to Sword-Fight

By his death in 323 B.C., Alexander the Great had created one of the world's largest empires. Although the military tactics that he developed are more than 2,000 years old, they are still taught at military colleges around the world. At an early age, Alexander learned the skills a soldier of his time needed, including how to ride a horse, shoot a bow, and throw a spear.

Read a Biography

DIRECTIONS: *A biographer is someone who writes about someone else's life. Alexander's most famous present-day biographer is Harold Lamb. The selection that follows is from Harold Lamb's book,* Alexander of Macedon: The Journey to World's End. *In the following selection, Alexander and his classmate Ptolemy are practicing their sword-fighting in front of their instructor. Read the selection, and answer the questions that follow.*

"But Ptolemy fought viciously, carefully, easily managing to keep ahead of Alexander in the count of blows scored on the wooden shield. Clearly he showed that he was superior [to Alexander] in skill. Then, at times, he hurt Alexander . . . flicking the sword blade suddenly against his thigh or the side of his head, to draw blood and induce the [instructor] to stop the fight. Then Ptolemy would smile, as if tired of playing with such toys.

"Once the [instructor] had not stopped the sword-fight between the boys, and Alexander found himself limping so that he could barely shift his weight from one foot to the other, and blood running into his eyes half blinded him. He tried to shake the blood clear of his eyes; instead Ptolemy's face shone through a red haze, and suddenly the coldness went out of Alexander. His sword felt light, his arm moved free, and his legs drove him forward. Behind the red veil Ptolemy's shield was breaking, and his sword wavered helplessly.

"Alexander felt the fierce warmth of a headlong hunt, when he pressed close upon a weakened deer. Then he heard the [instructor] shouting, 'Rest!' and [the instructor's] spear knocked the swords apart. Ptolemy was sobbing and staggering about, badly hurt.

"The [instructor] held fast to Alexander's right arm and walked him away, until he quieted. 'If you can't master that temper,' he growled, 'you won't live long.'

"To Philip [Alexander's father] the [instructor] made a different report. 'He is incredibly fast, and he is much more dangerous than the others. But . . . he loses his head. I doubt if he will ever learn to use weapons as he should.' "

(Continued)

Use after reading Chapter 7, Lesson 4, pages 229–233.

Harcourt Brace School Publishers

1. Do you think Alexander and Ptolemy were good friends? Explain your answer.

no; because they fought against each other so viciously

_____

_____

2. What do you think is meant by the phrases "Ptolemy's face shone through a red haze"

and "Behind the red veil"? that Alexander was looking through the blood covering his eyes

_____

_____

3. What do you think is meant by the phrase "and suddenly the coldness went out

of Alexander"? that he forgot about his pain and became more aggressive

_____

_____

4. Why do you think Ptolemy reminded Alexander of a weakened deer?

Like a weakened deer, Ptolemy was ready to be overtaken.

_____

_____

5. Why do you think the instructor gave Alexander's father a different report from

what he actually said to Alexander? He did not want Alexander to remember that he had won

the match, but rather that he had lost his temper, and that in battle, that could cost him his life.

_____

_____

ANCIENT GREECE

Connect Main Ideas

DIRECTIONS: Use the organizer to show that you understand how the chapter's main ideas are connected. Complete the organizer by writing two examples to support each main idea.

Early Peoples of Greece
Different cultures came to control ancient Greece.

1. Students' answers should include
_____
mention of the ancient Minoans and
_____
Mycenaeans.

2. _____
_____
_____

City-States and Greek Culture
The people of ancient Greece developed different ways of life.

1. Students' answers should include
_____
mention of Sparta and its emphasis on
_____
a military society and Athens and its
_____
democracy.

2. _____
_____
_____

Ancient Greece

The Golden Age of Athens
Periods of war and peace affected the ways of life of ancient Greeks.

1. Students may mention that the Persian
_____
Wars brought Greeks together while the
_____
Peloponnesian War tore them apart.

2. The peace between the two wars offered
_____
Athens a time of great achievement.
_____
_____

Alexander's Great Empire
Alexander the Great changed the Mediterranean region forever.

1. Students may mention the extent of
_____
Alexander's empire, the spread of Greek
_____
culture, and the achievements of

2. Hellenistic mathematicians, geographers,
_____
and scientists.
_____
_____

Use after reading Chapter 7, pages 210–235.

NAME _____ DATE _____

ROMAN GOVERNMENT

Use an Organizational Chart

**DIRECTIONS: In 753 B.C. Roman government began as a monarchy. By 494 B.C.
Rome was a republic. The structure of that republic is shown below. Use your
textbook to help you complete the blanks in the diagram and the questions.**

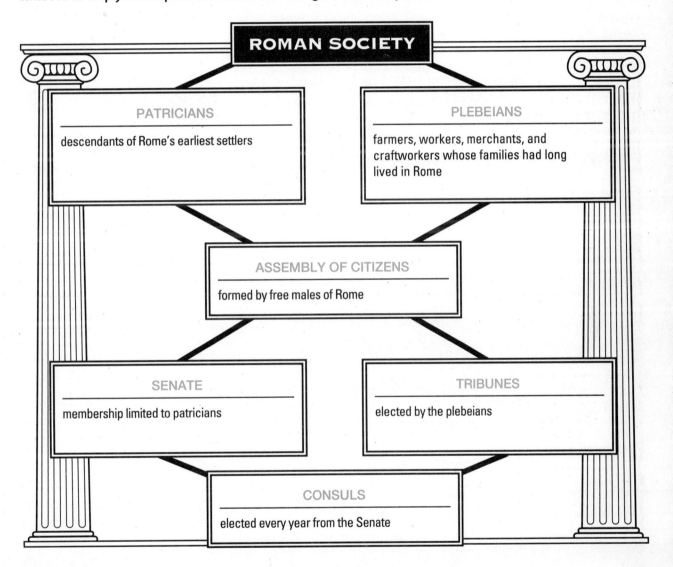

ROMAN SOCIETY

PATRICIANS
descendants of Rome's earliest settlers

PLEBEIANS
farmers, workers, merchants, and
craftworkers whose families had long
lived in Rome

ASSEMBLY OF CITIZENS
formed by free males of Rome

SENATE
membership limited to patricians

TRIBUNES
elected by the plebeians

CONSULS
elected every year from the Senate

1. How many consuls were elected from the Senate? two _____

2. How many tribunes were elected? ten _____

3. What was the primary power of the tribunes? They could veto Senate laws. _____

4. What special action could Romans take in an emergency? They could appoint a dictator
for a six-month term.

NAME _____ DATE _____

THE ROMAN EMPIRE

Break Information into Small Pieces

DIRECTIONS: It is easier to learn material in smaller pieces. This lesson has four sections, each of which is listed below. Use your textbook to answer the questions under each section.

Rome Becomes an Empire

1. What event left Rome without a leader? the death of Julius Caesar

2. What significant event happened in 31 B.C.? Octavian defeated Antony and Cleopatra and gained leadership of all Roman lands.

3. Who was Rome's first true emperor? Octavian (Augustus)

The Age of Augustus

1. What was the *Pax Romana*? a time of peace and unity for Rome

2. Give an example of a law passed by the Romans. A person is innocent until proven guilty; people cannot be forced to speak against themselves in a court of law.

3. What was the purpose of the first Roman census? to let the government know how many people were in the empire, so that all could be taxed

4. What was the main purpose of the Roman road system? to allow quick movement of Roman legions from province to province

Pride in Rome

1. What is a basilica? a huge marble building often used for government

2. What was the name of Rome's largest arena? the Colosseum

3. What is an aqueduct? a combination of bridges and canals that carry water from place to place

Literature, Arts, and Language

1. What is meant by the phrase "Conquered Greece conquered its uncultured conqueror and brought the arts to Rome"? The Romans, who had conquered Greece, copied Greek culture. They borrowed Greek ideas for architecture, art, writing style, and philosophy.

2. What language became common throughout the Roman Empire? Latin

Use after reading Chapter 8, Lesson 2, pages 243–247.

Harcourt Brace School Publishers

NAME _____ DATE _____

HOW TO COMPARE Historical Maps

Apply Map Skills

DIRECTIONS: Use the two maps on this page to answer the questions that follow.

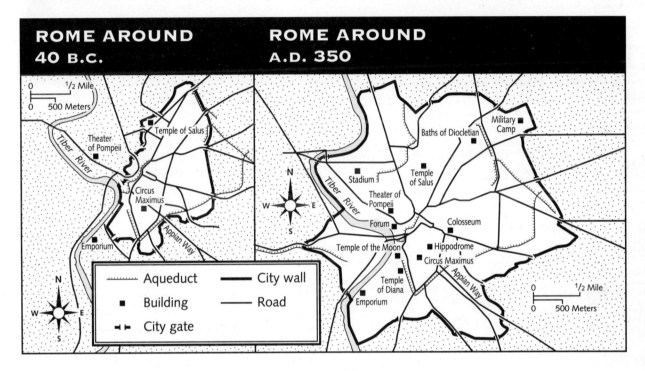

ROME AROUND 40 B.C.

ROME AROUND A.D. 350

Temple of Salus
Theater of Pompeii
Tiber River
Circus Maximus
Appian Way
Emporium

Military Camp
Baths of Diocletian
Stadium
Temple of Salus
Theater of Pompeii
Tiber River
Forum
Colosseum
Temple of the Moon
Hippodrome
Circus Maximus
Temple of Diana
Emporium
Appian Way

Aqueduct   City wall
Building   Road
City gate

0   1/2 Mile
0   500 Meters

1. How many years apart are these two maps? ____390 years____

2. What physical feature is common to both maps? __the Tiber River__

3. In 40 B.C. was the Theater of Pompeii inside or outside the city wall? __outside__

4. In A.D. 350 was the Stadium inside or outside the city wall? __inside__

5. In 40 B.C. how many openings were there in the wall? __15__

   in A.D. 350? __18__

6. What formed most of the western boundary of Rome in A.D. 350? __the Tiber River__

Harcourt Brace School Publishers

NAME _____ DATE _____

Ranks in the United States Army

☆ ☆ ☆ ☆ ☆ ☆

Read a Table

DIRECTIONS: In the Learn with Literature lesson, you read about Sextus Duratius, a professional soldier in a Roman legion. Sextus hoped that one day he might be promoted to the rank of senior centurion, about the same as a captain in the United States army today. The table that follows shows the ranks and symbols worn by officers in the United States army. Use this chart to answer the questions that follow.

RANK	SYMBOL	RANK	SYMBOL
General (color–gold)	★★★★	Lieutenant Colonel (color–silver)	
Lieutenant General (color–gold)	★★★	Major (color–gold)	
Major General (color–gold)	★★	Captain (color–silver)	
Brigadier General (color–gold)	★	First Lieutenant (color–silver)	
Colonel (color–silver)		Second Lieutenant (color–gold)	

1. What is the highest rank in the United States army? general _____

2. What insignia represents the rank of colonel? silver eagle _____

3. Which is a higher rank, captain or major? major _____

4. Which rank is represented by two silver bars? captain _____

Use after reading Chapter 8, Lesson 3, pages 250–252.

Harcourt Brace School Publishers

NAME _____ DATE _____

ROME

Create an Outline

DIRECTIONS: *One good way to summarize a body of information is to provide an outline of it. You may recall that in an outline, you can use Roman numerals (I, II, III), capital letters (A, B, C), Arabic numerals (1, 2, 3), and lowercase letters (a, b, c). Below is an outline that has been partially filled in. Use your textbook to complete this outline by filling in the missing titles of the subsections and other facts for the first lesson of the chapter. On a separate sheet of paper, create an outline for the remaining lessons of the chapter. Use the Lesson 1 outline as a guide.*

I. Chapter 8: Ancient Rome

  A. Lesson 1: The Roman Republic

    1. The Peninsula of Italy

      a) The peninsula of Italy looks like a high-heeled boot.

      b) The hills and mountains of Italy are less rugged than those in Greece. _____

    2. The Founding of Rome

      a) The rolling land around Rome offered fertile soil for farming.

      b) Rome was founded in 753 B.C.

    3. From Monarchy to Republic _____

      a) Etruscans took control of Rome about 600 B.C. _____

      b) Patricians had more rights than plebeians.

    4. The Path of Roman Conquest

      a) Hannibal was the general of the army of Carthage. _____

      b) Lands under Roman rule were divided into provinces. _____

    5. From Republic to Dictatorship _____

      a) In 83 B.C. Lucius Sulla became dictator over all of Rome.

      b) In 45 B.C. Julius Caesar became dictator over all of Rome. _____

HOW TO READ A Telescoping Time Line

Apply Time Line Skills

DIRECTIONS: The time line below shows some of the key dates in the history of ancient Greece and the Roman Empire. One section of the time line has been expanded to show some dates that could not have been shown at the scale of the main time line. Use these two time lines to complete the following questions.

TELESCOPING TIME LINE

776 B.C.   Greeks hold first Olympic Games — 800 B.C.

753 B.C.   Rome founded — 700 B.C.

600 B.C.

509 B.C.   Rome establishes a republic — 500 B.C.

432 B.C.   Construction of Parthenon completed — 400 B.C.

146 B.C.   End of last Punic War — 300 B.C.

200 B.C.

45 B.C.   Assassination of Julius Caesar — 100 B.C.

27 B.C.   Beginning of the Roman Empire — 0

A.D. 79   Pompeii destroyed

A.D. 80   Construction of Colosseum completed — A.D. 100

A.D. 200

A.D. 313   Constantine makes Christianity an accepted religion of the Roman Empire — A.D. 300

A.D. 330   Byzantium renamed Constantinople

A.D. 410   Goth leader Alaric attacks Rome — A.D. 400

Expanded section

340 B.C. — Alexander becomes king of Macedonia

335 B.C. — Alexander defeats Persians at Tyre and Gaza

330 B.C. — Alexander defeats Persians at Gaugamela

Alexander defeats Persians at Persepolis and Bactra-Zauspa

325 B.C. — Death of Alexander the Great

320 B.C.

Harcourt Brace School Publishers

(Continued)

Use after reading Chapter 8, Skill Lesson, page 259.

1. When was Rome founded? 753 B.C. _____

2. In what year did Alexander defeat the Persians at Bactra-Zauspa?
   330 B.C. _____

3. What event in Roman history took place 18 years after the assassination of Julius Caesar?
   beginning of the Roman Empire _____

4. Which was completed first, the Colosseum or the Parthenon?
   the Parthenon _____

5. How long after Alexander became king of Macedonia did he die?
   13 years _____

6. When did the last Punic War end? 146 B.C. _____

7. When was Byzantium renamed Constantinople?
   A.D. 330 _____

8. Could the destruction of Pompeii have been caused by the Goth attacks on Rome?
   Explain your answer. no; because the Goth attacks came after the destruction of Pompeii _____

   _____

9. Which part of the time line has been expanded with a larger scale?
   the part dealing with the military campaign of Alexander the Great in the Persian Empire; the part

   from 340 B.C. to 320 B.C. _____

   _____

10. Why is the telescoping time line helpful? Without it, the information showing Alexander's _____

    military campaigns would have to be condensed into too small a space.

    _____

    _____

Ancient Rome

Connect Main Ideas

DIRECTIONS: Use the organizer to show that you understand how the chapter's main ideas are connected. Complete the organizer by writing two details to support each main idea.

The Roman Monarchy and Republic
Over the years the forms of government in Rome changed.

1. _Students may mention Rome's shedding of Etruscan rule and its monarchy, the beginning of_ _the Roman Empire, and the eventual change to a dictatorship._

2. _____

Ancient Rome

The Roman Empire
Many people united under the Roman Empire.

1. _Students may mention that many cultures united as one, the role of Roman roads in_ _connecting people, and the importance of the Latin language._

2. _____

Religion and the Roman Empire
Christianity spread through the Roman Empire and changed Roman life.

1. _Students may mention the beginning of Christianity, the ways Christianity grew, the people_ _who helped bring growth to Christianity, the acceptance of Christianity in the empire, and_ _the growing belief in one God._

2. _____

Harcourt Brace School Publishers

Use after reading Chapter 8, pages 236–261.

THE MOSAIC *of* HISTORY

Recognize General and Supporting Statements

DIRECTIONS: In the three boxes below are general statements describing the Byzantine Empire. Underneath, there are 11 supporting facts. Write the number of each supporting fact in a block beneath the general statement it supports.

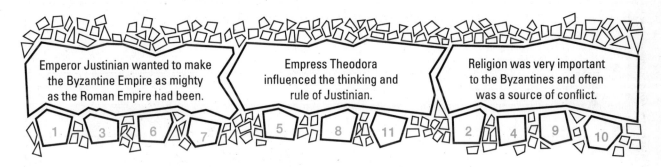

Emperor Justinian wanted to make the Byzantine Empire as mighty as the Roman Empire had been.

Empress Theodora influenced the thinking and rule of Justinian.

Religion was very important to the Byzantines and often was a source of conflict.

1 3 6 7   5 8 11   2 4 9 10

1. Justinian expanded trade to build up the Byzantine economy.

2. Disagreements over the use of icons contributed to the split between Christians in the Byzantine Empire and those in western Europe.

3. Justinian set out to conquer lands that Rome had lost.

4. Justinian wanted the Byzantine people to follow orthodox, or officially accepted, Christianity.

5. Theodora encouraged Justinian to make laws that were more fair to women.

6. Justinian wrote a code of law that organized and adapted the Roman codes of law.

7. Justinian built roads, bridges, and aqueducts to make Constantinople a "New Rome."

8. Theodora suggested that Justinian choose Belisarius as general of the Byzantine army.

9. The church of Hagia Sophia in Constantinople was the largest and most beautiful church in the world.

10. A large section of the Justinian Code dealt with church matters.

11. Justinian was once able to put down a rebellion because of the courageous advice of Theodora.

HOW TO DETERMINE POINT OF VIEW

The Byzantine Empress Theodora never forgot that she was once poor and that she and her sisters had to work in the circus to escape starvation. Later, Theodora took up acting. As empress she helped poor women to better themselves. She also worked to allow people to follow forms of Christianity other than the empire's official version.

Apply Thinking Skills

DIRECTIONS: *Below are several laws from the Justinian Code. Put an X on the line next to each one that reflects Theodora's point of view. Explain your choices on a separate sheet of paper.*

___X___ **51.** People who employ female stage performers may not force them to promise to continue in this work. Women who have taken an oath to continue as performers will be doing their duty to God by breaking it. Employers inducing a woman to take such an oath are to be heavily fined, and the fine is to go to the woman to help her start a new and more moral way of life.

___X___ **94.** We have thought it necessary to amend the law that requires mothers, when about to become guardians of their own children, to swear on oath that they will not enter into a second marriage.

_____ **109.** Wives who do not practice the official religion of the empire are not to enjoy all the privileges enjoyed by women who do practice the official religion of the empire.

___X___ **117.** After providing for their children as required by the law, mothers and grandmothers may leave their property and other wealth to anyone that they choose.

_____ **122.** Artisans, laborers, and sailors are forbidden to demand or accept increases in wages. Offenders are to pay the treasury three times the amount concerned.

___X___ **130.** When soldiers pass through a city, the cost of feeding and housing them should not be placed upon any citizen of the community.

Use after reading Chapter 9, Skill Lesson, page 280.

THE FIVE PILLARS OF ISLAM

Muslims follow five basic rules of faith. These rules come from the Qur'an and are called the Five Pillars of Islam.

Use Primary Sources

DIRECTIONS: Look at the Five Pillars of Islam. Then read the statements from the Qur'an below. In each statement, find and underline a key word or phrase that connects it with one of the pillars. Then write the letter of each statement in the correct pillar

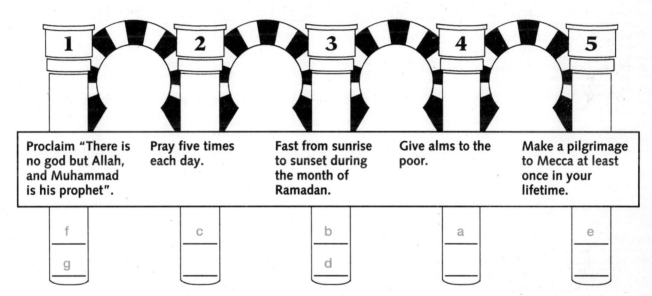

1	2	3	4	5
Proclaim "There is no god but Allah, and Muhammad is his prophet".	Pray five times each day.	Fast from sunrise to sunset during the month of Ramadan.	Give alms to the poor.	Make a pilgrimage to Mecca at least once in your lifetime.
f	c	b	a	e
g		d		

Statements from the Qur'an

a. "The righteous man . . . gives his wealth to his kinsfolk, to the orphans, to the needy, to the wayfarers and to the beggars. . . ." (2:177)

b. "Eat and drink until you can tell a white thread from a black one in the light of the coming dawn. Then resume the fast till nightfall. . . ." (2:186)

c. "Stay at your prayers in the mosques." (2:186)

d. "Allah . . . desires you to fast the whole month so that you may magnify Him and [give] thanks to Him for giving you His guidance." (2:184)

e. "Make the pilgrimage and visit the Sacred House for His sake. Allah is aware of whatever good you do." (2:196–197)

f. "Allah: there is no god but Him, the Living, the Eternal One. Neither slumber nor sleep overtakes Him." (2:255)

g. "As for those that have faith, . . . they are the heirs of Paradise." (11:20)

SPEAKING FOR Myself

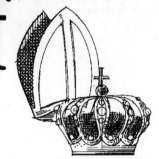

Distinguish Between Fact and Opinion

DIRECTIONS: Below are statements that could have been made by eight different people living in medieval Europe. Decide who the speaker is for each statement, and write the identifying letter on the first line in front of the statement. Then decide whether the person is stating a fact or an opinion. Write F for fact or O for opinion on the second line.

___d___ ___O___ **1.** Everyone knows that I'm the best farmer ever to set foot in a field on this manor. It's not fair that I can't own land myself.

___a___ ___F___ **2.** The nobles forced me to sign the Magna Carta.

___g___ ___O___ **3.** It is God's will that we take the holy city of Jerusalem back from the Seljuk Turks, and I will join with others to do so.

___e___ ___F___ **4.** In 1095 I called for all of Christendom to regain access to the holy places and to make them safe for Christians to visit.

___c___ ___F___ **5.** My sworn duty as vassal of the king is to provide soldiers for his army, to collect taxes, and to serve as he requires.

___b___ ___O___ **6.** Our meetings, called the Fields of May, are very exciting. The nobles who gather with me gain valuable knowledge to help them lead the people wisely.

___f___ ___F___ **7.** On Christmas Day in the year 800, I crowned Charlemagne "Emperor of the Romans."

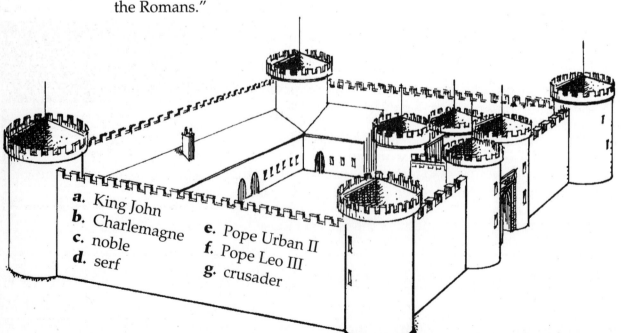

a. King John
b. Charlemagne
c. noble
d. serf
e. Pope Urban II
f. Pope Leo III
g. crusader

Harcourt Brace School Publishers

NAME _____ DATE _____

HOW TO UNDERSTAND World Symbols

Apply Thinking Skills

DIRECTIONS: Read the information about coats of arms, and use crayons or markers to fill in the correct colors on Charlemagne's coat of arms, shown at right. Then answer the question below.

The background was called the **field,** and its color was described using these words:

gules (red)	argent (white)
sable (black)	azure (blue)
or (yellow)	vert (green)

The design on the field was called the **charge.** Geometric designs were often used. Popular symbols were:

- Lion—strength and nobility
- Eagle—symbol of the Roman Empire
- Griffin—mythical beast with the upper body of an eagle and the lower body of a lion
- Cross of Christ—symbol of Christianity
- Fleur-de-lis—stylized lily, symbol of the Virgin Mary and emblem of the kings of France

What do you think is the significance of Charlemagne's coat of arms?

The eagle was the symbol of the Roman Empire.

The fleur-de-lis was the symbol of the kings of

France. Charlemagne was both king of the

Franks and emperor of the Romans.

CHARLEMAGNE'S COAT OF ARMS	
LEFT SIDE	**RIGHT SIDE**
Field—or	**Field**—azure
Charge: Eagle's claws and beak— gules Eagle's eye—argent Eagle's body—sable	**Charge:** Fleurs-de-lis—or

Use after reading Chapter 9, Skill Lesson, page 294–295.

A Knight in Shining Armor

Apply Information

DIRECTIONS: Read the following information about the use of armor in northern Italy during the Middle Ages. Then label the various parts of the knight's armor in the illustration on the next page.

Until the thirteenth century, armor consisted of chain mail, made from iron links or steel rings. The *hauberk* was a long shirt of chain mail that covered a soldier's body.

To provide more protection and comfort, metal plates that covered specific parts of the body became part of the armor. Their smooth, rounded surfaces helped guide the tip of an enemy's sword away from the knight. Since a knight on horseback could easily be wounded in the legs by foot soldiers, metal plates called *poleyns* were added to fit over the knees. Later, *greaves* were added to protect the shins and *cuisse* to protect the thighs. The foot guards, called *sabaton*, had overlapping plates so the knight could move his foot naturally.

A cone-shaped helmet was called a *bascinet*, and a mail cape, or *camail*, fastened to the bascinet protected the neck and shoulders. Some bascinets had hinged *visors* to protect the face. The first *gauntlets* were leather gloves, but these were replaced by metal plates on the hand and wrist and by scales on the fingers. Eventually knights wore *breastplates* and backplates over the hauberk for added protection.

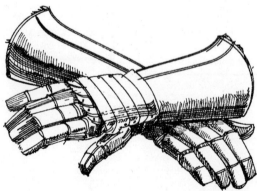

(Continued)

Use after reading Chapter 9, Lesson 4, pages 296–301.

North Italian Knight
About 1380–1390

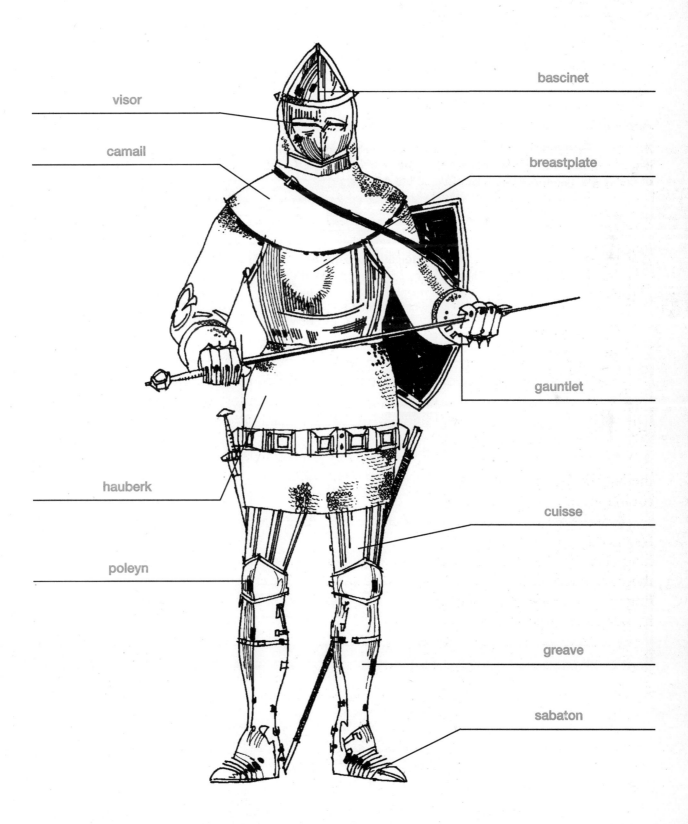

bascinet

visor

camail

breastplate

gauntlet

hauberk

cuisse

poleyn

greave

sabaton

Harcourt Brace School Publishers

Use after reading Chapter 9, Lesson 4, pages 296–301.

Heirs of ROME and PERSIA

Connect Main Ideas

DIRECTIONS: Use this organizer to show that you understand how the chapter's main ideas are connected. Complete the organizer by writing three examples to support each main idea.

Heirs of Rome and Persia

The Byzantine Empire
Byzantine emperors built on their Roman past while making needed changes.

1. Students may mention copying of Roman building style, Justinian's

2. revision of Roman laws, and conquering of lands Rome had lost.

3. _____

The Muslim Empire
The religion of Islam affected people living in the lands into which it spread.

1. Students might mention that many people in the lands accepted Islam,

2. and they began to live according to the Five Pillars of Islam.

3. _____

Europe in the Middle Ages
Individuals and groups affected governments and ways of life during the Middle Ages in Europe.

1. Students might mention Charlemagne, vassals and serfs, knights, and

2. crusaders.

3. _____

Use after reading Chapter 9, pages 274–303.

THE
Golden Age
OF
CHINESE POETRY

Learn from Primary Sources

DIRECTIONS: Two of the most talented poets of the Tang dynasty were Li Bo and Tu Fu. Read their poems on this page. Then answer the questions on the next page.

Li Bo

Poem 1
Life in the World is but a big dream;
I will not spoil it by any labor or care.

Forever committed to carefree play.
We'll all meet again in the Milky Way.

Poem 2
hand to hand, swords flashing
men grapple and die in the field
horses fall, their squeals
drift skyward

. . . .

What have the generals accomplished?
what they know
is less than what we've learned—

a sword's a stinking thing
a wise man will use
as seldom as he can.

Tu Fu

Poem 3
I remember in my fifteenth year
    my heart was still childish:
Strong as a brown calf, I ran to and fro.
When pears and dates ripened in the
    country in the eighth month,
In a single day I could climb the trees
    a thousand times.

Poem 4
women like goddesses
are dancing inside
all silk and perfume
guests in sable furs
music of pipes and fiddles
camel-pad broth being served
with frosted oranges
    and pungent tangerines.

behind those red gates
meat and wine are left to spoil
outside lie the bones
of people who starved and froze
luxury and misery a few feet apart!
My heart aches to think about it.

(Continued)

Use after reading Chapter 10, Lesson 1, pages 305–309.

1. How would you describe Li Bo's attitude in Poem 1? carefree _____

_____

2. What can you learn about warfare in China in the eighth century from Li Bo's second poem?
They used swords and rode horses. There was close contact during combat.

3. What lesson did Li Bo think the generals should have learned?
They should have seen that fighting accomplishes nothing.

_____

4. If you were Li Bo, what title might you give Poem 2? Why? Accept all reasonable responses.

_____

5. Can you see anything in Tu Fu's poems to suggest that life had changed since he was a youth? Use examples from his poems to support your answer.
As a boy, he could get fresh fruit just by climbing the trees. Later the fruit seems to be available

only to rich people.

_____

6. What details in Tu Fu's second poem tell you that the people inside are rich?
silk, perfume, sable furs, more food than they can eat

_____

7. If you were Tu Fu, what title might you give Poem 4? Explain your answer.
Accept all reasonable responses.

_____

8. Do you think a Golden Age in any country is "golden" for all the people?
Use the poems to explain your answer. There are probably always some people who have to

pay the price for the prosperity of others, including soldiers who fight and die to protect the country.

The upper class lives differently from the lower class.

_____

Harcourt Brace School Publishers

Culture SHOCK

When the Mongol Empire conquered all the lands from eastern Europe to the Pacific Ocean, it created a trade bridge to China. As a result, Europe, Mongolia, and China interacted and changed.

Understand Cause and Effect

DIRECTIONS: Read the following list of causes. Then, from the list at the bottom of the page, find the effect that was a likely outcome of each cause, and write the letter of the cause on the line next to the effect.

Causes

a. The Chinese had been using navigational compasses for more than 200 years before Marco Polo saw them.

b. Marco Polo reported how the Chinese used gunpowder for catapult bombs and fire arrows.

c. Marco Polo's book, *The Travels of Marco Polo*, created great desire in Europe for Chinese goods.

d. Marco Polo brought fine porcelain from China to Europe.

e. The Mongols realized that agriculture and technology were the sources of China's wealth.

f. Marco Polo's return to Venice in 1295 inspired seafaring countries to search for a sea route to China.

Effects

___f___ In 1514 the first Portuguese trading ship reached China.

___b___ Armies in Europe began to experiment with cannons about 1340.

___c___ Chinese cities became busy trading centers, supplying Europe with goods.

___a___ European sailors and explorers used Chinese-type compasses.

___e___ The Mongols promoted Chinese civilization and stopped raiding and destroying as they had at first.

___d___ Europe began importing porcelain but did not learn the secret of making it until 500 years later.

Harcourt Brace School Publishers

Precise, STROKES
CLEAN

Find Clues in Reading

DIRECTIONS: Read the thoughts of a 12-year-old Japanese boy in the short story below. Use the clues in it and what you have learned in your textbook to answer the questions that follow the story.

I learn to write like other Japanese children. It's hard work, but it's fun, too. Each letter must be precise, graceful. Each is made with one clean stroke—without hesitation. My father, who loves writing and poetry, says it is an art to write with brush and ink. He says it takes the same concentration to write that it takes to wield a sword. That's why writing a poem or enjoying a pretty garden is just as important as being accomplished with a sword. I guess that's why he always says, "Practice the arts of peace on the left hand, and the arts of war on the right." I promise him I will—not just because he says so, but because I want to be like him when I grow up. Next year, when I am 13, I will shave the front part of my head.

1. What title might you give to this story?

Accept all reasonable responses. _____

2. What do you think the boy's father meant when he said that it takes the same

concentration to write that it takes to wield a sword? To do anything well takes practice

and commitment. _____

3. Do you think gardening is important in this boy's life? Why?

yes, because he equated the writing of a poem with the enjoyment of a pretty garden

_____

4. What do you think is the meaning of a boy having the front part of his head shaved

at the age of 13? It is a sign that he is grown up and is ready to take his place as a man.

_____

INCA Record Keeping

Learn from an Artifact

DIRECTIONS: Read the following paragraph, and study the drawing on the right. Then answer the questions that follow.

The Incas had no written language or numbers. Instead, they recorded important information on string devices known as quipus (KEE•pooz). The colors and twists of the grouped strings designated what was being counted. The knots showed the totals. The Incas based their method of counting on a decimal system like ours. The number *0* was indicated by the lack of a knot. This system of keeping records required a special class in Inca society of trained quipu interpreters.

1. What kinds of things do you think would have to be counted in a society such as

the Incas had? Responses may include population, tax payments, food production, storage,

and distribution.

2. Why do you think people would have to be specially trained to read and keep

records using quipus? It was a complicated system that would take a long time to learn and lots

of practice to remember.

3. What quality of the Incas do you think use of the quipu indicates?

They had to be highly organized, logical thinkers.

4. To communicate with the people, the Inca ruler sent out messengers.
How do you suppose the runners carried the ruler's decrees and orders?

Without a written language, they would have had to memorize his decrees and pass them along to

other runners who did the same.

Harcourt Brace School Publishers

NAME _____ DATE _____

HOW TO USE Maps with Different Scales

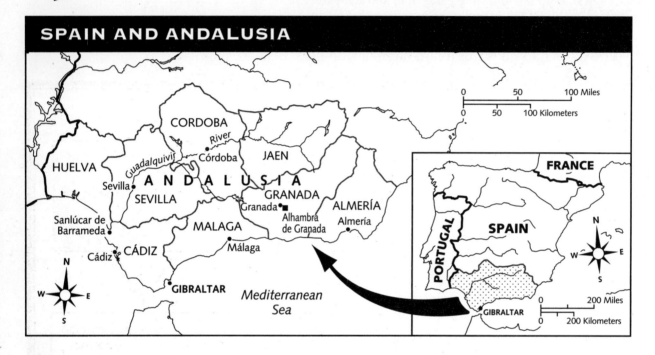

SPAIN AND ANDALUSIA

CORDOBA
River
Guadalquivir Córdoba
HUELVA
Sevilla A N D A L U S I A JAEN
SEVILLA GRANADA
Granada ALMERÍA
Sanlúcar de Alhambra Almería
Barrameda MALAGA de Granada
Cádiz CÁDIZ Málaga
N
W E
S
GIBRALTAR Mediterranean
Sea

0   50   100 Miles
0   50   100 Kilometers

FRANCE
PORTUGAL SPAIN
N
W E
S
GIBRALTAR
0   200 Miles
0   200 Kilometers

Apply Map Skills

DIRECTIONS: Look at the main map of Andalusia and the inset map of Spain and Portugal. Then answer the questions below in the space provided. On a separate sheet of paper, explain each of your answers.

_____*main*_____ **1.** Which map is better for measuring the distance between Gibraltar and Sanlúcar de Barrameda?

_____*inset*_____ **2.** Which map is better for measuring the distance between Gibraltar and the French border?

_____*main*_____ **3.** Find the Alhambra de Granada, which was a palace and military stronghold of the Moors. Which map did you use to find it?

_____*$2\frac{1}{4}''$*_____ **4.** About how many inches are used to show 200 miles on the main map?

_____*$\frac{1}{2}''$*_____ **5.** About how much space is needed to show 200 miles on the inset map?

_____*80 mi.*_____ **6.** About how many miles is it between Granada and Córdoba?

Use after reading Chapter 10, Skill Lesson, pages 326–327.

Harcourt Brace School Publishers

Empires in Asia and the Americas

Connect Main Ideas

DIRECTIONS: Use this organizer to show that you understand how the chapter's main ideas are connected. Complete the organizer by writing three details to support each main idea.

Growth for China
Under Sui, Tang, and Song rulers, China developed a rich culture.

1. Students may mention the Grand Canal and

2. other improvements of the Sui, the Tang's

3. Golden Age and the achievements in poetry, and the Song's fine cities.

Empires in Asia and the Americas

The Mongol Empire
The Mongols brought the Chinese into closer contact with other cultures.

1. Students may mention that the Mongols pro-

2. vided safety for traders and encouraged trade

3. with Marco Polo and others.

Japanese Culture
The Japanese borrowed from and adapted Chinese culture.

1. Students may mention that the Japanese bor-rowed Chinese law,

2. dress, architecture, art, manners, writing, and ways of governing.

3. _____

Civilizations in the Americas
People living in the Americas between 1100 and 1500 adapted to and changed their environment.

1. Students may mention the Aztecs' changes to the physical environ-

2. ment at Tenochtitlán, the Aztecs' chinampas, the Incas' roads and

3. terraces, and the Mississippians' mounds.

Life in MEDIEVAL *Africa*

Leo Africanus was born in Spain, and in 1510 he traveled to the Songhay cities of Gao, Jenné, and Timbuktu. His book about his experiences was called *History and Description of Africa and the Notable Things Contained Therein.*

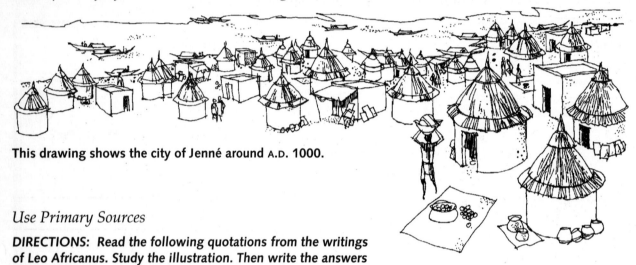

This drawing shows the city of Jenné around A.D. 1000.

Use Primary Sources

DIRECTIONS: Read the following quotations from the writings of Leo Africanus. Study the illustration. Then write the answers to the questions on the next page.

In Gao, the capital:

"Whosoever will speak unto the king must first fall down before his feet, and then taking up the earth must sprinkle it upon his own head and shoulders."

"It is a wonder to see what plenty of merchandise is daily brought hither (here), and how costly . . . things [are]. Horses bought in Europe for ten ducats (coins) are sold again for forty and sometimes fifty ducats apiece."

". . . spices also are sold at a high rate: but of all other commodities salt is most extremely dear."

In Jenné:

". . . a city prospering from its crops of rice, barley, fish, cattle, and cotton. The cotton is a major crop sold unto the merchants of Barbary. . . ."

(Continued)

Use after reading Chapter 11, Lesson 1, pages 341–347.

In Timbuktu:

"There are numerous judges, doctors, and clerics, all receiving good salaries from the king. . . . [Books and manuscripts brought here] . . . are sold for more money than any other merchandise."

"Here are many shops of [craftworkers] and merchants . . . and hither do the Barbary merchants bring cloth of Europe. All the women of this region except the maid servants go with their faces covered. . . . The inhabitants, and especially strangers living there, are exceedingly rich, insomuch that the king married both his daughters unto two rich merchants."

1. What was the significance of the Songhay custom for greeting the king?

It humbled the visitor and acknowledged the king's authority.

_____

_____

2. Africanus reported that the king "pays great respect to men of learning." What evidence does he give to support that statement?

Educated people, such as judges, doctors, and clerics, were supported by the king; books were

_____

very valuable.

_____

3. What does Africanus say about the women in Songhay? Women, except for servants,

covered their faces when they went to the marketplace.

_____

4. Besides gold, what did the Songhay have to offer traders? crops, especially cotton

_____

_____

5. Why was trade so profitable? Traders received much more for a product than they paid for it.

_____

_____

6. In the drawing on the previous page, you can see traditional round African houses. What architectural influence of Mediterranean civilizations do you also see?

rectangular, flat-roofed houses

_____

7. Traders came to Jenné on overland trade routes through the Sahara. What other means of trade does the drawing show?

boats for trading on a river

_____

HOW TO COMPARE MAPS
WITH DIFFERENT PROJECTIONS

Apply Map Skills

DIRECTIONS: Study the four map projections shown below. Then in the table on the next page, place check marks in the columns that match the descriptions of the map features in the left column.

ROBINSON

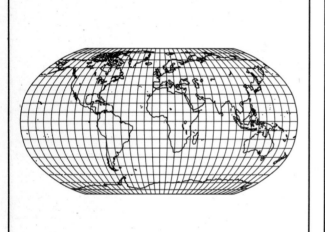

VAN DER GRINTEN

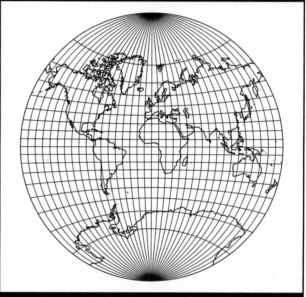

POLAR

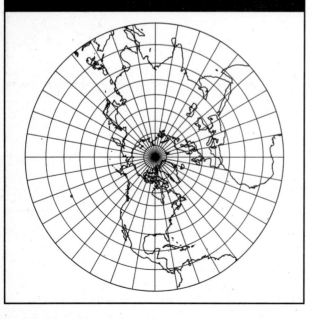

ORTHOGRAPHIC

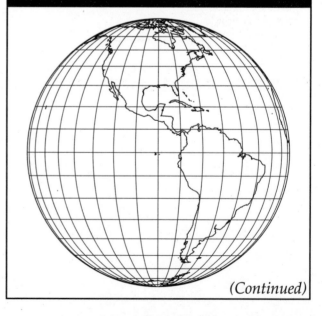

(Continued)

NAME _____ DATE _____

	ROBINSON	VAN DER GRINTEN	POLAR	ORTHOGRAPHIC
The map looks most like a globe.				✓
The map looks as if it were drawn looking down on the North Pole.			✓	
The North Pole is shown as a point.		✓	✓	✓
The North Pole is shown as a line.	✓			
The map can show only one hemisphere.			✓	✓
Lines of latitude are parallel to each other.	✓		✓	✓
Antarctica is shown much larger than it really is.	✓	✓		
The equator passes through the center of the map.	✓	✓		✓
The equator forms the circumference of the map.			✓	
The map is the best one to use for planning an airplane trip between Japan and the United States.			✓	

Travel—Then and Now

During the Middle Ages, more people traveled than ever before. Some were traders or merchants. Some were pilgrims. Travel was often dangerous and uncomfortable.

Draw Analogies to Experiences

DIRECTIONS: Below are quotations from two famous travelers, Ibn Battuta and Marco Polo. Match their travel descriptions with features of present-day travel listed in the box below, and write the letters in the blanks. Letters may be used more than once.

f   "At every halting place [in China under the Mongols] there is a [hotel supervised] by an officer. . . . Every evening after sunset . . . this officer visits the inn accompanied by his clerk; he takes down the name of every stranger who is going to pass the night there, seals the list, and then closes the inn door upon them. In the morning he comes again with his clerk, calls everybody by name, and marks them off one by one."   *Ibn Battuta*

c   The government [of Persia] has ordered ". . . payment of two or three groats [type of coin] for each loaded beast according to the length of the journey. . . ."   *Marco Polo*

e   The officer ". . . then dispatches along with the travelers a person whose duty it is to escort them to the next station. . . ."   *Ibn Battuta*

e   "The government . . . at the request of the merchants shall supply good and efficient escorts from district to district for their safe conduct. . . ." *Marco Polo*

DIRECTIONS: Using the same list of present-day travel features, match each of the following words that refer to medieval travel with its present-day travel equivalent.

d trade routes   b oasis   a caravansaries

g journals of travelers   h maps

PRESENT-DAY TRAVEL FEATURES			
a. motels	**c.** toll payment	**e.** highway patrol	**g.** guidebooks
b. rest area	**d.** interstate highways	**f.** motel check in/check out	**h.** road atlas

Use after reading Chapter 11, Lesson 2, pages 351–355.

Harcourt Brace School Publishers

TRACKING THE SILK ROAD

Map Skill *Plot a Route*

DIRECTIONS: *Most of the places described in the selection The Silk Route are shown on the map below by a city symbol and a number. Review the literature selection and study the map called A World of Trade. Then, using the clues below, label the cities where the caravan stopped. Finally, connect all the caravan stops of the trip, in order, from Chang'an to Byzantium.*

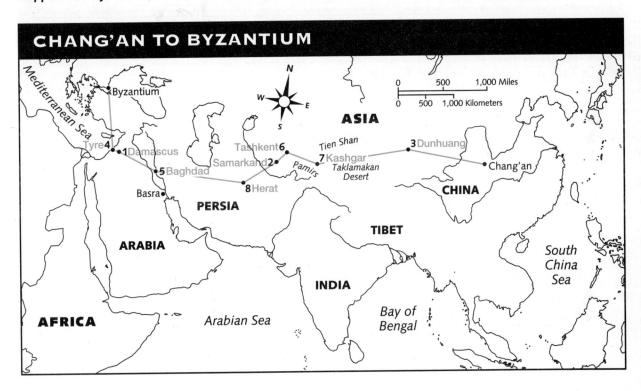

CHANG'AN TO BYZANTIUM

1. Damascus   located northwest of Baghdad and east of Tyre

2. Samarkand   stop between Tashkent and Herat

3. Dunhuang   religious center

4. Tyre   port on the Mediterranean Sea

5. Baghdad   ships can reach it by traveling upriver from the port of Basra

6. Tashkent   located at the eastern edge of the Persian culture world

7. Kashgar   an oasis that was famous for its fruits

8. Herat   located at what was then the eastern edge of the Islamic world

OVERLAND Trade

Connect Main Ideas

DIRECTIONS: Use the organizer to show that you understand how the chapter's main ideas are connected. Complete the organizer by writing three details to support each main idea.

Overland Trade

The Trading Empires of West Africa
The peoples of West Africa grew strong through trade with others.

Trade Routes Linking Asia and Europe
Unified empires led to trade among the peoples of Africa, Asia, and Europe.

1. Students may mention the Sonenke trade, Ghana's gold trade, and Mali's rich trading markets.
2. _____
   _____
3. _____
   _____

1. Students may mention the Muslim Empire and its trade routes, the Mongol's protection of the Silk Road, and new markets that opened to both the
2. Muslims and the Mongols as they expanded their
3. empires.

Use after reading Chapter 11, pages 340–365.

The Voyages of
ZHENG HE

After the Mongols' defeat, China wanted the world to recognize its power, its superior culture, and its control of the trade routes. To accomplish this, Admiral Zheng He was chosen to make a series of ocean voyages.

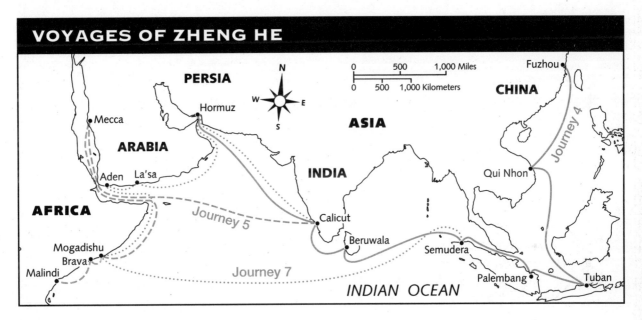

VOYAGES OF ZHENG HE

Understand Map Routes

DIRECTIONS: *The box below lists the main cities visited on three of Zheng He's journeys. Select a different color for each journey shown in the box. Show that journey's color in the appropriate space in the box. Then, using those colors, draw the paths of the three journeys on the map.*

JOURNEY 4 ▪		JOURNEY 5 ▪		JOURNEY 7 ▪	
1. Fuzhou	5. Semudera	1. Calicut	4. Brava	1. Semudera	4. La'sa
2. Qui Nhon	6. Beruwala	2. Mecca	5. Malindi	2. Mogadishu	5. Hormuz
3. Tuban	7. Calicut	3. Mogadishu		3. Aden	6. Calicut
4. Palembang	8. Hormuz				

Harcourt Brace School Publishers

The MEDITERRANEAN Sea

Map Skill *Place Events in Time and Place*

DIRECTIONS: Using information in your textbook, match the events on the right with the centuries on the left and write the correct letter in the blank.

_a_ **1.** sixth century   **a.** The Mediterranean and the Black seas are brought under Byzantine rule.

_d_ **2.** seventh century   **b.** Venice takes control of most Byzantine lands on the eastern coast of Mediterranean Sea.

_e_ **3.** tenth century   **c.** The Ottoman Turks take control of Constantinople.

_b_ **4.** thirteenth century   **d.** The Muslims take control of Cyprus.

_c_ **5.** fifteenth century   **e.** The Byzantines regain control of Cyprus and Crete.

DIRECTIONS: Find and label the following places on the map below:

Adriatic Sea	Constantinople	Florence	Pisa
Africa	Crete	Genoa	Strait of Gibraltar
Amalfi	Cyprus	Mediterranean Sea	Venice
Black Sea			

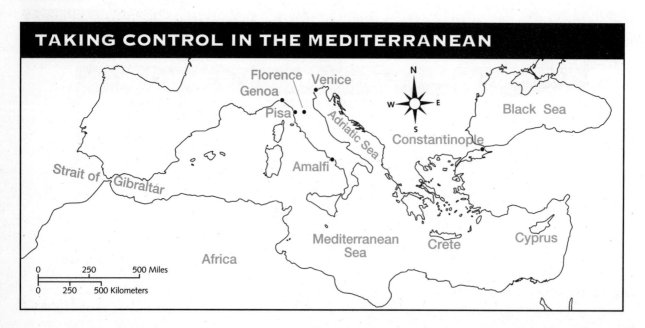

TAKING CONTROL IN THE MEDITERRANEAN

    Use after reading Chapter 12, Lesson 2, pages 372–375.

HOW TO COMPARE INFORMATION IN CIRCLE GRAPHS

Apply Graph Skills

DIRECTIONS: *Examine the two circle graphs below. Then answer the questions on the next page. The first graph shows the distribution of United States exports to Japan in 1992. The second shows United States imports from Japan in 1992. The information in both graphs is presented in United States dollars.*

U.S. EXPORTS TO JAPAN

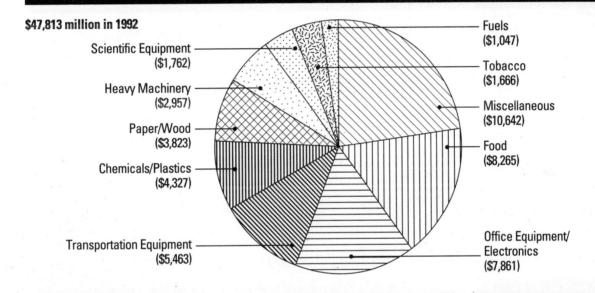

$47,813 million in 1992

Scientific Equipment ($1,762)
Heavy Machinery ($2,957)
Paper/Wood ($3,823)
Chemicals/Plastics ($4,327)
Transportation Equipment ($5,463)

Fuels ($1,047)
Tobacco ($1,666)
Miscellaneous ($10,642)
Food ($8,265)
Office Equipment/ Electronics ($7,861)

U.S. IMPORTS FROM JAPAN

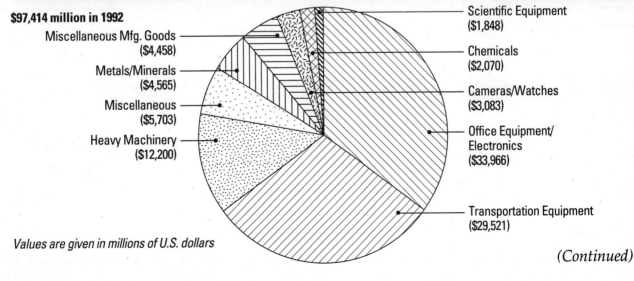

$97,414 million in 1992

Miscellaneous Mfg. Goods ($4,458)
Metals/Minerals ($4,565)
Miscellaneous ($5,703)
Heavy Machinery ($12,200)

Scientific Equipment ($1,848)
Chemicals ($2,070)
Cameras/Watches ($3,083)
Office Equipment/ Electronics ($33,966)
Transportation Equipment ($29,521)

Values are given in millions of U.S. dollars

(Continued)

NAME _____ DATE _____

1. Which country exports more to the other? Japan exports more to the United States.

   By about how much? Japan's exports to the United States are approximately twice the value
   of U.S. exports to Japan.

2. Not counting the miscellaneous category, which U.S. export to Japan is worth the
   largest dollar amount? food

   What is the total value of that export? $8.265 billion

3. Which category of Japanese export to the United States is worth the largest
   dollar amount? office equipment/electronics

   What is the total value of that export? $33.966 billion

4. About what percent of U.S. exports to Japan is made up of scientific equipment?
   4 percent

5. About what percent of U.S. imports from Japan is made up of
   transportation equipment? 30 percent

6. What do you think is included in transportation equipment?
   cars, trucks, and parts for cars and trucks

7. Which country do you think is more likely to want to place a high tax on imported goods?
   the United States

   Explain your answer. It would make imports so costly that fewer goods would be imported.

Use after reading Chapter 12, Skill Lesson, pages 376–377.

Harcourt Brace School Publishers

Do You Speak VIKING?

Because Vikings eventually settled in England, the English language picked up some Viking words. Some of the words you use today came from old Norse, the language of the Vikings.

Decode Runes

DIRECTIONS: Runes are sticklike letters that Vikings used for writing. The Viking alphabet did not have a rune for every sound in English. We have added five runes (in brackets) to the runic alphabet for easier translation. Translate the runic words below to find six English words that came from the Vikings.

RUNIC ALPHABET

f u th a r k h n i a s t b m l R [e] [g] [c] [w] [y]

l e g

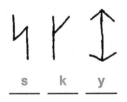

s k y

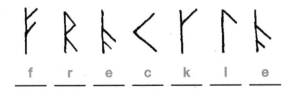

f r e c k l e

e g g

l a w   b e r s e r k

Harcourt Brace School Publishers

Use after reading Chapter 12, Lesson 3, pages 378–381.

HOW TO FORM A Logical Conclusion

Apply Thinking Skills

DIRECTIONS: Examine the following facts about Viking family life. Use this information to find the most likely conclusion for each question, and circle the correct letter.

List of Facts

- Grandparents, parents, children, uncles, aunts, and cousins lived together.

- Feuds among different families were common.

- After about age ten, boys often lived with foster families. Sometimes foster families were relatives, but often the foster father and a boy's own father had been foster brothers. A boy and his foster family became very close.

- Boys and girls learned to do both men's and women's jobs. Both boys and girls learned to swim, ride horses, and use weapons.

- Viking men and women chose their own marriage partners. Women remained single if they chose.

- A woman was in charge of the household and took care of all business when her husband was away.

1. Why do you think Viking girls learned to ride, swim, and handle weapons?

   a. Women went on raids with the men.

   (b.) Women had to defend their farms when their husbands were away.

   c. Many women were not married and had to defend themselves.

2. Why do you think Viking boys went to live with foster families?

   (a.) Foster families gave them additional support if there was a feud.

   b. The natural parents had taught them all they could.

   c. There was not enough room for them at home.

3. What could you conclude about the status of Viking women?

   a. Women carried the most authority in Viking society.

   b. Viking women had few rights.

   (c.) Women were treated with respect.

Use after reading Chapter 12, Skill Lesson, page 382.

Harcourt Brace School Publishers

THE FORMATION OF AN ATOLL

Apply Information

DIRECTIONS: Read the description about the formation of a coral atoll. Key words are underlined. Label the three illustrations using the underlined key words.

An island can form in a single day when a volcano pushes up from beneath the sea. Atolls, too, start with a volcano, but atolls take thousands of years to create.

During the first stage of atoll formation, a volcano pushes up from the sea and creates a <u>volcanic island</u>. Then a coral reef grows in the <u>ocean</u> around the volcanic island. It is called a <u>fringe reef</u>. In the second stage, the <u>volcano erodes and sinks slowly</u>, just inches a year. At the same time, the coral grows a few inches a year. By the time the volcano is half sunken, the coral looks like a halo of land surrounding a small island. Between the halo and the island is a <u>lagoon</u>. At this stage, the reef is called a <u>barrier reef</u>. In the final stage, the <u>volcano disappears</u> beneath the ocean, leaving a ring-shaped reef. The coral is still growing, and the <u>lagoon is shallow</u>. At this stage, the reef is called an <u>atoll</u>. In time, sand builds up on the atoll, and plants start to grow.

STAGE ONE	STAGE TWO	STAGE THREE
volcanic island	volcano erodes and sinks slowly	volcano disappears
ocean	lagoon	lagoon is shallow
fringe reef	barrier reef	atoll

Use after reading Chapter 12, Lesson 4, pages 383–387.

NAME _____ DATE _____

Sea and River Trade

Connect Main Ideas

DIRECTIONS: Use the organizer to show that you understand how the chapter's main ideas are connected. Complete the organizer by writing two details to support each main idea.

Indian Ocean Trade
Trade around the Indian Ocean linked many peoples.
1. Students may mention Muslim sea travelers to East Africa, India, and China and the East African trading ports.

2. _____

The Mediterranean and the Black Seas
Some city-states became leaders of trade in the Mediterranean and Black seas.
1. Students may mention the city-states of Venice, Pisa, Genoa, Milan, and Florence and tell of their role in Mediterranean sea trade.

2. _____

Sea and River Trade

The Northern Seas
Two important trading cultures developed in Northern Europe.
1. Students should mention the Vikings and the members of the Hanseatic League.

2. _____

Conquering the Pacific
People solved problems to explore and settle the islands in the Pacific Ocean.
1. Students may mention as problems fear of the unknown, opinions against sea travel, and unsuitable ships. Students also may state that every inhabitable Pacific Island became settled.

2. _____

Harcourt Brace School Publishers

Use after reading Chapter 12, pages 366–389.

Art and SCIENTIFIC METHOD

During the Renaissance, people looked at things in new ways. Scientific methods were not used just for science. Artists, for instance, used these methods to create a new and better kind of paint.

Apply Knowledge to a New Situation

DIRECTIONS: *Imagine that you are an artist in the 1400s who wants to develop a new paint. Read the list below of steps to create your paint. Then read the list of steps in a scientific method. On the line for each step in a scientific method, write the letter or letters of the appropriate steps to create a new paint.*

STEPS TO CREATE A NEW PAINT

a. I have mixed a variety of pigments collected from sea shells, chamomile, charcoal dust, and powdered mushrooms with oil. I have used olive oil and linseed oil.

b. I have noticed that some dyes can stain almost anything—fabrics, stone, skin, even teeth.

c. Most of the pigments mixed well with either oil. But I found that linseed oil worked better. The colors are good—rich and bright. The paint takes a long time to dry. I can work carefully and even rework the scene if necessary.

d. Our method of painting frescoes on fresh plaster allows no room for error. If a mistake is serious, I have to replaster the wall and start over.

e. It should be possible to make a paint that does not fade and that dries slowly enough to allow an artist to work carefully.

f. Frescoes fade and crumble with time.

Steps in Scientific Method	Steps to Create New Paint
1. Observe the facts.	b, d, f
2. Formulate a hypothesis.	e
3. Experiment to see if the hypothesis is true.	a
4. Accept or modify the hypothesis.	c

THE HIGH PRICE OF WOOL

Recognize Cause and Effect

DIRECTIONS: Shown at the right are some results of the increased demand for wool. Below is a series of boxes. Fill in the boxes by putting the results in the correct order to show the connections, or causes and effects, for these events.

Tenant farmers are forced to leave the land.

City people and newcomers suffer from low wages, job shortages, and crowding.

Tenant farmers seek work in cities in order to survive.

Nobles turn farms into pastures for sheep.

Prices in the wool trade rise sharply.

Prices in the wool trade rise sharply.
_____
_____

Nobles turn farms into pastures for sheep.
_____
_____

Tenant farmers are forced to leave the land.
_____
_____

Tenant farmers seek work in the cities in
_____
order to survive.
_____

City people and newcomers suffer from
_____
low wages, job shortages, and crowding.
_____

DIRECTIONS: Read the following quotation written by Sir Thomas More in 1516. On a separate sheet of paper, explain what you think More meant.

"Your sheep which are usually so tame . . . now devour human beings and [destroy] fields, houses and towns." (*Utopia, Book One*)

Use after reading Chapter 13, Lesson 2, pages 409–413.

Harcourt Brace School Publishers

NAME _____   DATE _____

HOW TO ACT AS A Responsible Citizen

Apply Thinking Skills

DIRECTIONS: Read the two paragraphs below. After you read each, check the boxes in front of the statements that you think describe how the person acted responsibly.

On December 1, 1955, a white man boarded a crowded bus in Montgomery, Alabama. The bus driver quickly ordered four African Americans to move back to make room for the white man. Three did. But Rosa Parks, a small, quiet woman, remained seated. She was already a worker for freedom for her people. She had always had faith that freedom was coming, but she had not planned on it being that day. The bus driver sent for the police. Rosa Parks was arrested and jailed. Later, the Supreme Court ruled that Alabama's segregated seating laws were unconstitutional. Rosa Parks's action that day inspired the struggle for civil rights for African Americans.

In 1952, Orville Redenbacher figured out how to increase the moisture content of popping corn so more kernels would pop. His popping corn produced a lower number of unpopped kernels. But it was also more expensive to make. The big popcorn manufacturers said it was too expensive. They said that people liked popcorn because it was a cheap snack, and they would not pay more for better pop-corn. Orville Redenbacher thought they would. He decided to try it himself. People bought his idea and his popcorn. Orville Redenbacher proved the large businesses wrong when his popping corn became the leading popping corn in America.

☐ Rosa Parks was a loud, pushy person.

☐ She did what was expected of her.

☑ She took a stand against what she thought was wrong.

☑ She believed in herself.

☑ She questioned the accepted way of doing things.

☑ Orville Redenbacher tested his ideas in science and in business.

☐ He was afraid to try something new.

☑ He believed in himself.

☑ He proved he was right by learning to make his idea work.

☐ He gave up when the experts and big companies rejected his idea.

Harcourt Brace School Publishers

Use after reading Chapter 13, Skill Lesson, page 414.

ACTIVITY BOOK   93

THE Santa Maria

In 1492 Christopher Columbus began a voyage in search of a new water route to Asia. He set sail aboard the *Santa Maria*, which was one of three ships that were part of the expedition.

Identify by Description

DIRECTIONS: Read the following description of the Santa Maria. The names of some parts of the ship have been underlined. On the next page is a cutaway illustration of the Santa Maria. Match the underlined words in the description below with the numbered parts of the ship by writing the words next to the corresponding numbers in the box beneath the drawing of the Santa Maria.

The captain's quarters were located in the highest room at the rear of the ship just beneath the afterdeck. In the middle of the captain's room was the pole of the mizzenmast. This pole went through all three decks like a huge spear and was firmly bolted into the keel at the bottom of the ship. On the deck below the captain's quarters, the helmsman could use the rudder. Food for the crew of the *Santa Maria* amounted to 1,200 gallons of wine, 2,400 pounds of fish and meat, and enough sea biscuits for two months at sea. This was stored in the cargo hold, a large area beneath the bottom deck. The mainmast, in the center of the ship, went down through two decks and was also built into the keel. It was much sturdier than either the light-weight foremast at the bow of the ship or the mizzenmast at the stern.

(Continued)

Use after reading Chapter 13, Lesson 3, pages 415–419.

Harcourt Brace School Publishers

Stern (Rear)

1. afterdeck	**5.** mainmast
2. captain's quarters	**6.** rudder
3. mizzenmast	**7.** keel
4. cargo hold	**8.** foremast

Use after reading Chapter 13, Lesson 3, pages 415–419.

New Directions for
EUROPE

Connect Main Ideas

DIRECTIONS: *Use the organizer to show that you understand how the chapter's main ideas are connected. Complete the organizer by writing three details to support each main idea.*

Changes in Europe
European government, society, and way of life changed.

1. Students should mention that new monarchies united their countries in Spain, France, and England; peasant farmers lost their lands to the land owners and moved to the cities to find work; and Martin Luther began a religious

2. reformation that split the Roman Catholic Church and divided the people of Europe.

3. _____

New Directions for Europe

Rebirth of Ideas in Europe
Changes in European thought encouraged individualism and creativity.

1. Italian merchants brought ideas from the East; these ideas spread to other countries. In art:

2. more lifelike works, use of perspective; In science: how the physical world works; in thought:

3. the importance of the individual. Some students may mention movable type, or specific figures such as Michelangelo, Galileo, Copernicus, and others.

Europeans Explore the Globe
European nations began to explore and claim lands overseas.

1. Factors students should mention: with the fall of Constantinople, traders lost their main route to Asia; governments and

2. merchants looked to the Atlantic Ocean for new routes to Asia; improvements in shipbuilding,

3. maps, and navigation made exploration of the Atlantic Ocean possible.

_____

Harcourt Brace School Publishers

Use after reading Chapter 13, pages 402–421.

NAME _____ DATE _____

FORCED MIGRATION

Gather Information from a Map

DIRECTIONS: Use the map below to answer the questions on the next page.

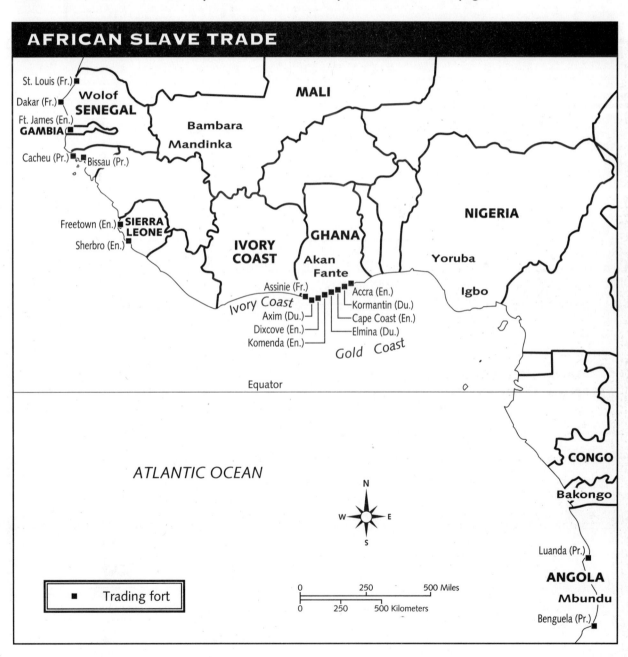

AFRICAN SLAVE TRADE

St. Louis (Fr.) ■
Dakar (Fr.) ■
Ft. James (En.) ■
GAMBIA ■
Cacheu (Pr.) ■ ■ Bissau (Pr.)

Wolof
SENEGAL

Bambara
Mandinka

MALI

Freetown (En.) ■ **SIERRA LEONE**
Sherbro (En.) ■

IVORY COAST

GHANA
Akan
Fante

NIGERIA

Yoruba

Igbo

Assinie (Fr.) ■
Ivory Coast
Axim (Du.) ■
Dixcove (En.) ■
Komenda (En.) ■

Accra (En.)
Kormantin (Du.)
Cape Coast (En.)
Elmina (Du.)

Gold Coast

Equator

ATLANTIC OCEAN

N
W ✦ E
S

CONGO

Bakongo

Luanda (Pr.) ■

ANGOLA
Mbundu

Benguela (Pr.) ■

■ Trading fort

0   250   500 Miles
0   250   500 Kilometers

Harcourt Brace School Publishers

(Continued)

Use after reading Chapter 14, Lesson 1, pages 423–428.   ACTIVITY BOOK   97

1. Each of the names of the trading forts on the map is followed by an abbreviation for the country that controlled the fort. Complete the table below by writing in the name of the country that is abbreviated.

ABBREVIATION	COUNTRY
En.	England
Pr.	Portugal
Fr.	France
Du.	Holland

2. The greatest number of slaves taken to the Americas came from the regions of the Congo and Angola. Who controlled trade there? the Portuguese

_____

3. Which two tribes do you think made up most of the slaves from the Congo and Angola?
the Mbundu and Bakongo

4. Many slaves taken to Georgia and the Carolinas came from the region of Sierra Leone. Who controlled trade there? the English

_____

5. Many trading forts were located along the Gold Coast. Which countries controlled these forts? England, France, and Holland

_____

6. Name seven African tribes north of the Equator from which slaves were taken.
Wolof, Mandinka, Bambara, Akan, Fante, Yoruba, and Igbo

_____

Harcourt Brace School Publishers

Use after reading Chapter 14, Lesson 1, pages 423–428.

The Conquest of Mexico

The conquest of Mexico from the Spanish point of view was recorded by Bernal Díaz del Castillo, who accompanied Hernando Cortés. It was also recorded by Bernardino de Sahagún, a Spanish Catholic missionary who arrived shortly after Cortés, in 1524. Sahagún learned Nahuatl, the Aztec language. He later wrote Aztec history, which included the Aztec view of the conquest.

Compare Historical Accounts

DIRECTIONS: Read the following quotations from two historical accounts of the conquest of Mexico. Compare what you read. Then answer the questions on the next page.

CANNONS

"And [the Aztecs] also asked what we did with those guns. . . . We answered that with stones placed in them we could kill whom we pleased, and that the horses, that ran like deer, could catch anyone we ordered them to. And Olintetl and the other chief men said, 'In that case, you must be gods.'" *Díaz*

"Moctezuma [Motecuhzoma] was shocked, terrified by what he heard. . . . how the great gun expelled the shot which thundered as it went off . . . in a shower of fire and sparks. . . . [Spanish] war gear, it was all iron. The animals they rode—they looked like deer—were as high as roof tops." *Sahagún*

ARMY

The Spanish army was "weary . . . ragged and sick" and had lost men to wounds, exposure, and illness. The soldiers "wondered what would happen to us when we had to fight Moctezuma if we were reduced to such straits by the Tlaxcalans." *Díaz*

"'We are not as strong as they,' was what they said as they described the Spaniards to [Moctezuma]. 'We are nothing compared to them.'" *Sahagún*

GOLD

"Such is the nature of us Spaniards that the more he told us [about the splendor of Tenochtitlán] . . . the more we longed to try our fortune." *Díaz*

The Spaniards' "thirst for gold was insatiable; they starved for it; they lusted for it; they wanted to stuff themselves with it as if they were pigs." *Sahagún*

(Continued)

MOCTEZUMA [Motecuhzoma]

Cortés promised the Indians "we would treat them as brothers and give them help against Moctezuma." *Díaz*

"When Moctezuma had finished his greeting . . . [Cortés] said, 'Let Moctezuma be at ease; he need not be frightened. We love him.'" *Sahagún*

1. What two things did the Spaniards bring that the Indians had not seen before?

guns and horses

2. How did the Spanish and Mexican armies view each other before they met?

Both thought that the other was more powerful.

3. What are two different ways of looking at the Spaniards' quest for gold?

that they were seeking their fortune or that they were greedy

4. Is there evidence that Cortés dealt honestly with the people of Mexico?

No. He said he would treat them like brothers, and that he loved Moctezuma. It was not true.

Use after reading Chapter 14, Lesson 2, pages 429–433.

HOW TO COMPARE INFORMATION ON MAPS

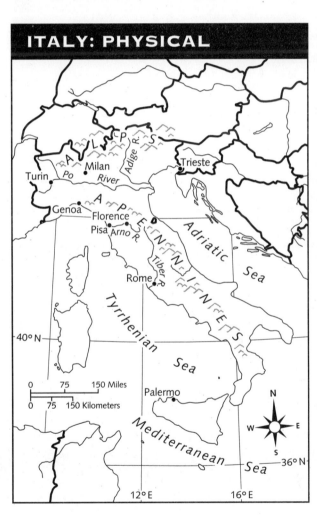

Apply Map Skills

DIRECTIONS: *Study the two maps of Italy below, then answer the questions on the next page.*

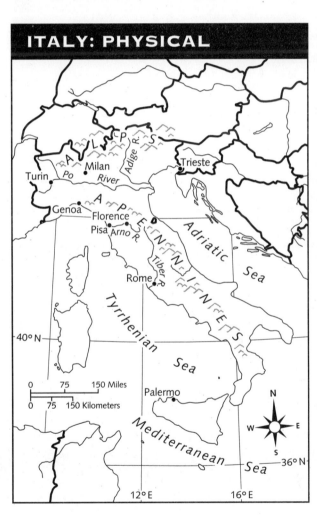
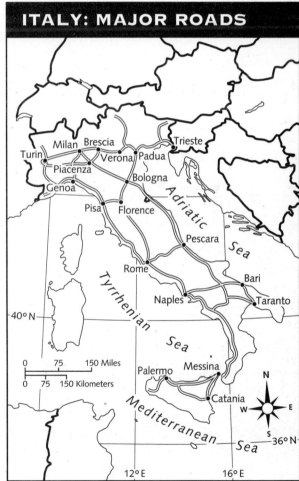

ITALY: PHYSICAL

ITALY: MAJOR ROADS

(Continued)

Use after reading Chapter 14, Skill Lesson, pages 434–435.

1. What kind of information does each map provide? Italy: Physical provides information about

mountains and rivers of Italy. Italy: Major Roads provides information about Italy's major roadways.

2. Which map would you use if you wanted to plan a trip from Turin to Bari?

Italy: Major Roads

3. In which direction would you travel on a trip from Turin to Bari?

southeast

4. Which map would you use if you were planning a boat trip on the seas and rivers of Italy?

Italy: Physical

5. What is the relationship between Italy's cities and mountains?

Most of Italy's cities are not in mountainous regions.

6. What is the relationship between the location of the roads and the mountains of Italy?

For the most part the roads run parallel to the mountains, rather than through them.

7. What do Rome, Florence, Pisa, and Turin have in common?

They are all located on rivers.

Use after reading Chapter 14, Skill Lesson, pages 434–435.

As told by an EYEWITNESS

Write a Report

DIRECTIONS: *Imagine that you are a young person who traveled on one of Columbus's ships as a cook's helper. Write a short report on your crew's landing and meeting with Morning Girl. In your own words, be sure to:*

- describe the island and how you felt when you saw land
- explain how you came to shore
- tell who you saw and describe her appearance
- tell how you knew she was friendly
- describe what you said and did
- explain your reaction to these new people

Students' descriptions of the island should resemble Morning Girl's [green palm trees, thick vegetation, red and yellow flowers, bright blue sky, brown sand, warm breeze]. They should express their excitement and surprise. They should describe Morning Girl as thin, wearing little or no clothing, with long hair. They may recall her wave [with fingers spread]. They may describe trying to communicate with Morning Girl and her people, perhaps eating with them. [Morning Girl indicates that this is what she thinks will happen and she mentions steamed fish. A cook's helper may tell how the food was prepared.] They should explain why the crew "seemed very worried, very confused, very unsure what to do next."

_____

_____

_____

_____

_____

_____

_____

Harcourt Brace School Publishers

HOW TO COMPARE
Information on
a Double-Line Graph

Apply Graph Skills

DIRECTIONS: The line graph below compares the population growth of China and the United States since 1950. Study the graph to answer the questions on the next page.

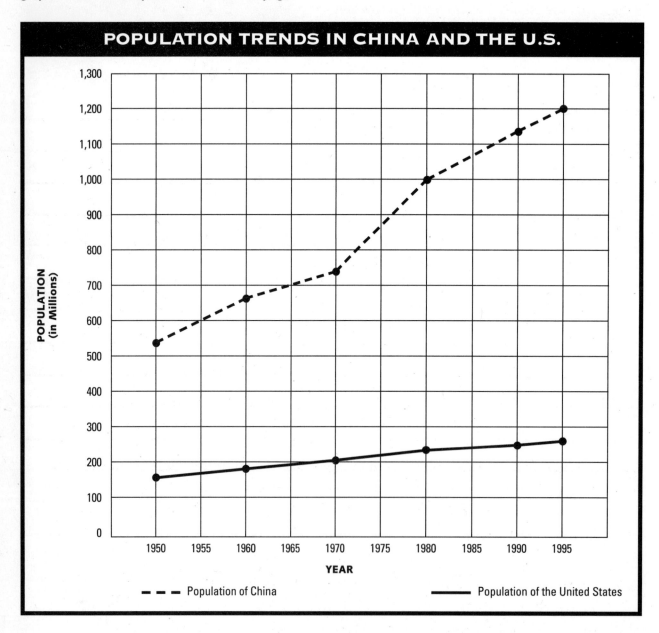

POPULATION TRENDS IN CHINA AND THE U.S.

- - - Population of China   ——— Population of the United States

Harcourt Brace School Publishers

(Continued)

Use after reading Chapter 14, Skill Lesson, pages 440–441.

1. If each horizontal line in this graph represents 100 million people, how many people are represented by a point halfway between two horizontal lines?

50 million
_____

_____

2. What was the population of China in 1990? about 1,133 million _____

_____

3. What was the population of the United States in 1990? about 250 million _____

_____

4. How can you tell, without looking at the numbers, which country has the faster

population growth rate? You can tell by the steepness of the line. _____

_____

5. Which country has the greater population growth rate? China _____

_____

6. Approximately how many years did it take China to double its 1950 population?

about 36 years
_____

_____

7. In which year did China reach a population of 1 billion? 1980 _____

_____

8. What was the population of the United States in 1980? 230 million _____

_____

9. About how many more people were living in China than in the United States in the

year 1995? about 930 million _____

_____

Harcourt Brace School Publishers

Europe, Africa, and the Americas Interact

Connect Main Ideas

DIRECTIONS: Use the organizer to show that you understand how the chapter's main ideas are connected. Complete the organizer by writing three details to support each main idea.

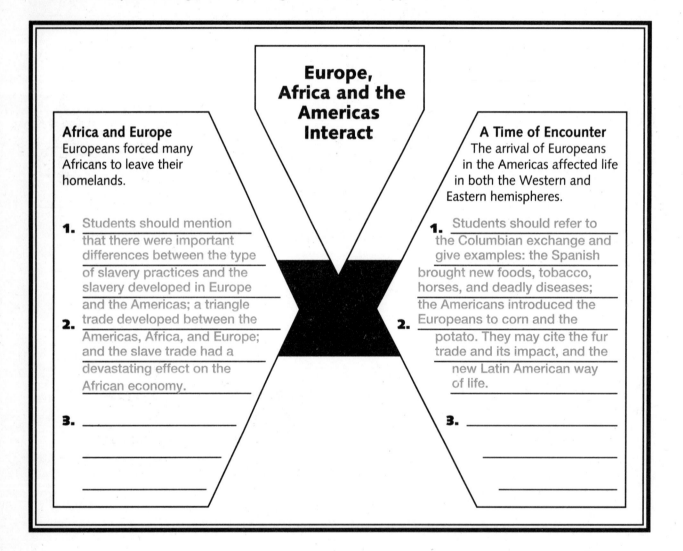

Europe, Africa and the Americas Interact

Africa and Europe
Europeans forced many Africans to leave their homelands.

1. Students should mention that there were important differences between the type of slavery practices and the slavery developed in Europe and the Americas; a triangle trade developed between the
2. Americas, Africa, and Europe; and the slave trade had a devastating effect on the African economy.

3. _____

A Time of Encounter
The arrival of Europeans in the Americas affected life in both the Western and Eastern hemispheres.

1. Students should refer to the Columbian exchange and give examples: the Spanish brought new foods, tobacco, horses, and deadly diseases; the Americans introduced the Europeans to corn and the
2. potato. They may cite the fur trade and its impact, and the new Latin American way of life.

3. _____

Use after reading Chapter 14, pages 424–443.

Harcourt Brace School Publishers

The Chinese Art of
CALLIGRAPHY

Calligraphy is the art of writing beautifully. For the Chinese, it is more than writing. It is art. The artist uses a soft, pointed brush to form Chinese characters on silk or paper. All strokes must be done gracefully and in the proper order.

Appreciate a Culture

DIRECTIONS: Use a felt-tipped marker or a small paintbrush and black ink. Try to draw each of the Chinese characters shown below.

This character means "tree" or "wood." Draw the strokes in order.

This character means "dog."

Now try the characters for the numbers "five," "six" and "seven."

Here is space for your try.

(Continued)

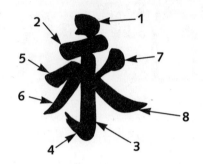

This character means "eternal." It contains eight directions of strokes of calligraphy. Try it, in the order indicated.

This character means "brilliant"!

Chinese artists "sign" their work with small seals. This tradition started during the Ming dynasty. The seals are always stamped with red ink. Here are three examples.

DIRECTIONS: *In this space design a seal using your name, initials, or a favorite symbol.*

Use after reading Chapter 15, Lesson 1, pages 445–449.

Süleyman's Military Campaigns

Trace Routes on a Map

DIRECTIONS: The table below shows 11 of Süleyman's campaigns. Use this information, on the map below the table, to draw a line connecting each of his military campaigns in the order that they happened.

1521 Belgrade	1529 Vienna	1534 Basra	1565 Malta
1522 Rhodes	1532 Güns	1541 Buda	1566 Szigetvár
1526 Mohács	1534 Baghdad	1548 Tabriz	

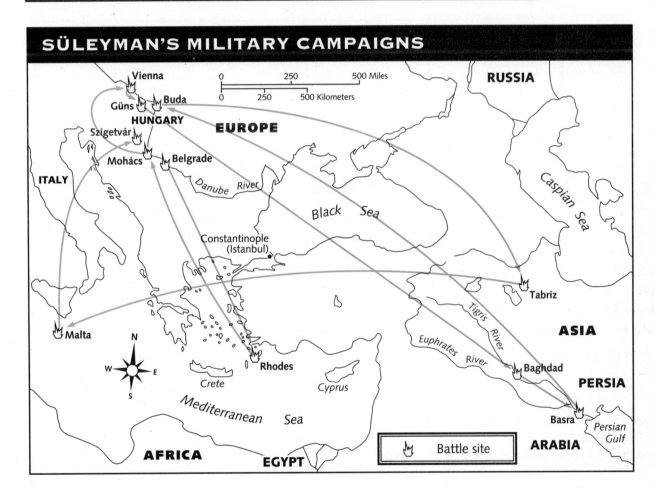

1. Can you identify any pattern in Süleyman's military campaigns?

Most of his battles were in eastern Europe.

2. What do you think Süleyman's motives might have been for some of these military actions?

He wanted to expand the Ottoman Empire toward western Europe.

Use after reading Chapter 15, Lesson 2, pages 450–454.

HOW TO READ A POPULATION PYRAMID

Apply Graph Skills

DIRECTIONS: Look at the population pyramid on this page. It shows the population of Zimbabwe. Compare the population patterns of Zimbabwe, the United States, and India, using this population pyramid and those in your text on page 455. Then answer the questions below.

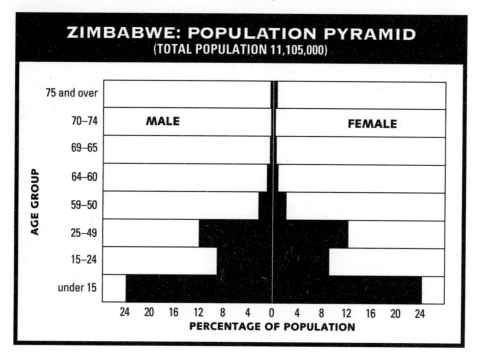

ZIMBABWE: POPULATION PYRAMID
(TOTAL POPULATION 11,105,000)

AGE GROUP

75 and over
70–74   MALE   FEMALE
69–65
64–60
59–50
25–49
15–24
under 15

24 20 16 12 8 4 0 4 8 12 16 20 24
PERCENTAGE OF POPULATION

1. Which is the largest population group in Zimbabwe? under 15 _____

2. How does this age group compare with the U.S. and India? It is a larger percentage than in either the U.S. or India. _____

3. Approximately what percentage of the total population of Zimbabwe is made up of people between the ages of 15 and 24? 19.5% _____

4. Are there more males or females who are 75 or over in Zimbabwe? more females _____

5. Which country has the highest life expectancy? the United States _____

6. What do you think might be some of the factors that affect life expectancy?
Possible answers include better health care, i.e. more doctors and hospitals, more nourishing food, healthy drinking water, more time for recreation.

Use after reading Chapter 15, Skill Lesson, page 455.

NAME _____ DATE _____

CHANGES IN ASIA

Connect Main Ideas

DIRECTIONS: Use the organizer to show that you understand how the chapter's main ideas are connected. Complete the organizer by writing two details to support each main idea.

China and Japan
The people of China and Japan changed their view of themselves in relation to the rest of the world.

1. Students may mention that both China and Japan turned away from trade with
outsiders; outsiders were still interested in trading with China; and shoguns

2. wanted to preserve Japan's unity and enforce the "closed country" policy.

Changes in Asia

The Ottoman and Mogul Empires
The policies of the Ottoman and Mogul empires affected the people they conquered.

1. Students may mention that the Ottoman empire brought peace, a fair
government, and advancements in learning; and that the Moguls allowed

2. Hindus to practice their own religion, and improved the economy of India.

Use after reading Chapter 15, pages 444–457.

A Tale of **Two Leaders**

Compare Historical Figures

DIRECTIONS: *Use information from your textbook to decide whether the descriptions in the right column below apply to George Washington, Napoleon Bonaparte, or both. Then in the left column, write Washington, Napoleon, or both.*

both	was a military leader
both	treated soldiers with respect
both	was respected by soldiers
Napoleon	was a dictator
Washington	led a meeting to plan a new, democratic government
Napoleon	crowned himself emperor
Washington	had the capital of a country named for him
Napoleon	invaded Russia
both	took part in ending a revolution
Napoleon	set up a code of laws

Use after reading Chapter 16, Lesson 1, pages 471–477.

HOW TO READ A Political Cartoon

Apply Visual Thinking Skills

DIRECTIONS: Examine the political cartoon below. Then answer the questions that follow it.

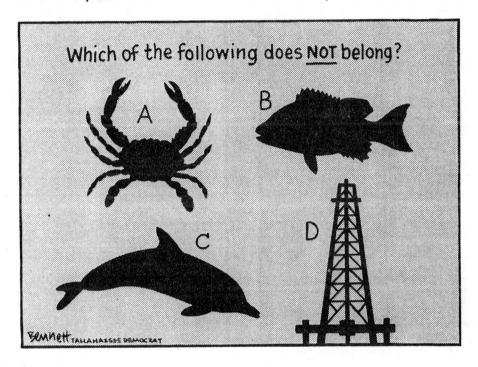

Which of the following does <u>NOT</u> belong?

A B C D

BENNETT TALLAHASSEE DEMOCRAT

1. Who drew this political cartoon? <u>Bennett</u>

2. Where did this political cartoon first appear? <u>in the *Tallahassee Democrat*</u>

3. What are the four items shown in the political cartoon?

crab, fish, porpoise, oil derrick

4. What do you think is the answer to the question raised in the political cartoon?

Explain your answer. <u>D, the oil derrick; all items are natural to the ocean except the oil derrick.</u>

5. What do you think the cartoonist's message is? <u>that drilling for oil should not be done in the</u>

ocean because the possible pollution could harm sea life

Simón Bolívar

Interpret Quotations

DIRECTIONS: The boxes below contain quotations from Simón Bolívar. Match each quotation with one of the explanations that follow, and write the letter of the explanation in the circle.

1815 (b)

To drive out the Spaniards and create a free government, what is needed is "union, obviously; but such a union will come about through sensible planning and well-directed actions. . . ."

1821 (d)

"You can be sure . . . that we are over . . . a volcano that is about to erupt. I fear peace more than war."

1821 (a)

I believe that we need . . . "a life-term president, with the power to choose his successor. . . ."

1830 (c)

"Fellow-Citizens, I am ashamed to say it, but independence is the sole benefit we have gained, at the sacrifice of all others."

---

a) A strong leader who will serve for life is needed in South America.

b) A union made through wise planning and good decisions will be needed to create a United States of South America.

c) Independence from Spain was won at high cost in lives and suffering, but real unity was not achieved.

d) The war for independence will not bring peace. Instead, new wars will violently erupt.

Harcourt Brace School Publishers

THE GROWTH OF DEMOCRACY

Connect Main Ideas

DIRECTIONS: Use the organizer to show that you understand how the chapter's main ideas are connected. Complete the organizer by writing three ways democracy grew for each main idea below.

The Growth of Democracy

Democratic Revolutions
Different types of leaders affected history in France and in what is now the United States during the late 1700s.

1. Students may mention Washington, who led the Continental Army; Jefferson, who wrote the Declaration of Independence; Bonaparte, who took control of the French government and created the Napoleonic Code; the

2. revolutionaries who spearheaded the French Revolution; Louis XVI, whose actions sparked the French Revolution; or the leaders who turned the French Revolution into a time of terror.

3. _____

_____

_____

_____

_____

Democratic Ideas in Latin America
The peoples of Latin America wanted changes in their governments.

1. Students may either list particular revolutionary leaders, such as Toussaint-Louverture in Haiti, José de San Martín and Simón Bolívar in South America, and Miguel Hidalgo in Mexico,

2. or give reasons for the changes, such as the structure of society in Latin America, the influences of the French and American revolutions, and the desire of the Creoles to control their own lives.

3. _____

_____

_____

_____

_____

Harcourt Brace School Publishers

NAME _____ DATE _____

What's Next???

Predict Likely Outcomes

DIRECTIONS: Three statements are listed for each of four categories below. Put a check mark in the box next to each statement that you think predicts the effect of technology in the future.
Accept all responses students can reasonably explain or defend.

1. AGRICULTURE

☐ Genetic engineers will develop crops that resist insects and make their own fertilizer.

☐ More food will be available, and world population will increase.

☐ Crops will be grown in controlled environments without using soil.

2. CITY LIFE

☐ Only small, zero-pollution cars will be allowed within cities.

☐ People will move out of cities, and cities will be used for business only.

☐ People will need computerized identification cards to move from one section of a city to another.

3. COMPUTERS

☐ Most people will speak to the computer instead of typing information with a keyboard.

☐ There will be a major reaction against computers, and many people will "pull the plug."

☐ People will use computers to order and pay for their groceries.

4. HEALTH

☐ Life expectancy will increase to 125 years.

☐ Tiny robots will swim through arteries to reach a problem area and do surgery.

☐ People will use handheld scanners to monitor their own body temperature, blood pressure, and general physical condition.

DIRECTIONS: On a separate sheet of paper, list at least one additional way that you think technology might make an impact on the future.

Use after reading Chapter 17, Lesson 1, pages 487–491.

Harcourt Brace School Publishers

HOW TO USE A Population Map

Map Skill *Apply Map Skills*

DIRECTIONS: Look below at the two maps of the world, and then answer the questions on the next page.

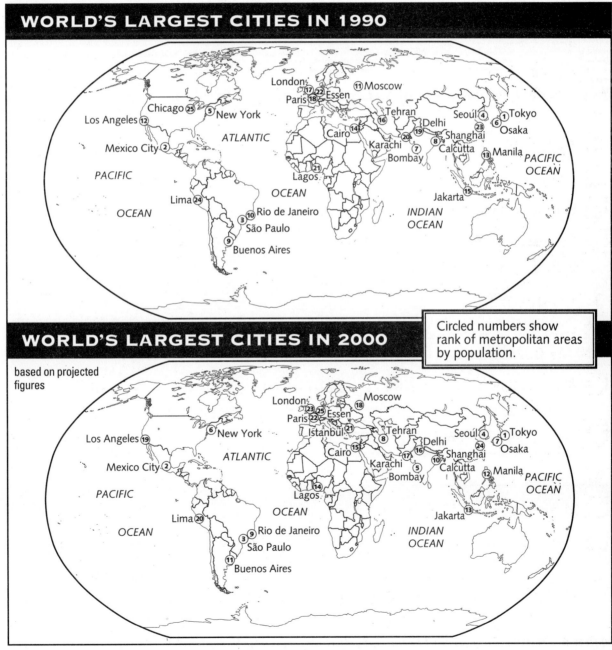

WORLD'S LARGEST CITIES IN 1990

Circled numbers show rank of metropolitan areas by population.

WORLD'S LARGEST CITIES IN 2000

based on projected figures

(Continued)

1. What were the five most populated cities in 1990?

Tokyo, Mexico City, São Paulo, Seoul, and New York

_____

_____

2. Which one of these five cities is not included among the five largest on the map of

population in the year 2000? New York _____

3. Which of the 25 most populated cities in 1990 were in the United States?

New York, Los Angeles, and Chicago

_____

_____

4. In 1990 what was the most populated city in Europe? Moscow _____

_____

5. Which of the 25 most populated cities in 1990 were in Europe?

Moscow, London, Paris, and Essen

_____

_____

6. On the map of cities in 2000, what is the most populated city in Africa?

Lagos

_____

7. According to the map, which city shows the greatest jump in population ranking from

1990 to 2000? Tehran _____

8. Based on the map showing cities in 1990, which continent do you think has the most

people? Explain your answer. Asia, because 11 of the metropolitan areas shown are in Asia

_____

_____

_____

NAME _____ DATE _____

A Day in the Life of a MILL WORKER

Read for Information

DIRECTIONS: Five blank lines are shown around the clock below. Using information from the story "The Clock", fill in the blanks to show some events during a typical day at the mill. Then answer the questions that follow.

mill wake-up bell rings
_____

work begins
_____

breakfast
_____

noon break for dinner
_____

quitting time
_____

1. How many hours did a mill worker work each day? twelve hours, with time out for

breakfast and dinner
_____

2. In what ways was Annie's work at home the same as her work at the mill?

In both places she had to twist the rolls of wool between her thumb and fingers onto the end of the

spinning yarn. She also had to be careful that the connection did not break.
_____

3. In what ways was Annie's work at home different from her work at the mill?

more walking at home; more noise at the mill; no time for tea breaks at the mill
_____

4. What were the advantages and disadvantages of working at the mill?

Advantages: Workers earned more money at the mill than they could at home. *Disadvantages:* The

workers could not take breaks or have a day off. They had to eat and rest on a strict schedule.
_____

Harcourt Brace School Publishers

Life in NEW HARMONY

Distinguish Between Fact and Opinion in Primary Sources

DIRECTIONS: The quotations below are from people who lived in or visited the community of New Harmony. Underline phrases or sentences that express the writer's opinion. Do not underline sentences that express fact.

"Mr. Jennings . . . delivered an excellent discourse on Equality. . . . [He said] that every person's worth should be measured by his capacity to be useful to his fellow beings."

"Mr. Fiquepal and Madam Fretageot [are] first rate teachers. . . . There are now at New Orleans on their way hither [here] a vast collection of books . . . In Harmony there will be the best library & the best School in the United States." *(from letters from William Pelham, resident and editor of the newspaper at New Harmony, to his son)*

"Mr. Jennings . . . intended, nevertheless, to leave this place again, and return back to Philadelphia. Many other members have the same design, and I can hardly believe that this society will have a long duration." *(from the published travel journal of Karl Bernhard, Duke of Saxe-Weimer)*

Use after reading Chapter 17, Lesson 3, pages 498–503.

The Beginning of the Industrial Age

Connect Main Ideas

DIRECTIONS: Use the organizer to show that you understand how the chapter's main ideas are connected. Complete the organizer by writing three details to support each main idea.

The Beginning of the Industrial Age

The Industrial Revolution
The new technology of the Industrial Revolution changed life in Britain and elsewhere.

1. Students may list key inventions, such as the iron plow, seed drill, steam engine, or power loom, and cite their impacts, or they may cite the effects of the Industrial Revolution, such as tex-

2. tiles changed from a cottage industry into a factory industry, countries established colonies in Asia and Africa to get resources for their growing industries, and industrial competition began

3. among countries.

_____

_____

_____

_____

Capitalism and Classes
Economic differences led to conflicts between social classes in Europe and the United States.

1. Students may mention the growth of the middle class, the resentment of the upper class by the middle class, the difficult conditions for the workers—which led them to explore labor unions and

2. socialism—or Marx and his ideas.

_____

_____

_____

_____

3. _____

_____

_____

_____

_____

FIVE NATIONAL FLAGS

Recognize National Symbols

DIRECTIONS: Read about each of the flags shown. Then color each flag as indicated.

UNITED STATES OF AMERICA

In 1777 the flag of the young United States had 13 stripes and 13 stars. Each stripe and each star represented one of the 13 original states. In 1818 Congress decided to keep the thirteen stripes and add a star for each new state. Today the U.S. flag has 50 stars.

WHITE
BLUE
RED
WHITE

FRANCE

Before the French Revolution in 1789, the national flag of France was plain white, the color of the reigning king. Earlier French flags were blue with the white or gold *fleur-de-lis.* The three colors of the present French flag represent the motto of the revolution—liberty, equality, and fraternity. Other countries borrowed the French colors or design when they gained independence.

BLUE	WHITE	RED

Harcourt Brace School Publishers

(Continued)

GREEN	WHITE	RED

ITALY

The design of Italy's flag was influenced by that of the French flag. The colors were established during the time Napoleon controlled part of Italy. After his defeat, the flag was not used until 1848, when it reappeared during the revolution led by Garibaldi. It became the flag of the kingdom of Italy, which was formed in 1861.

GERMANY

The black, red, and yellow flag of Germany dates from the time of the Napoleonic wars, 1796–1815. It was adopted as the national flag in 1848 by the first German parliament. In 1867 a black, white, and red flag designed by Prussian chancellor Bismarck was used. Since the unification of Germany in 1990, the black, red, and yellow flag has again flown over Germany.

BLACK
RED
YELLOW

JAPAN

The name *Japan* means "source of the sun," and the rising sun is a traditional symbol of the country. For centuries Japan had no national flag, partly because it was a closed country and avoided any outside contact. After Commodore Perry opened Japan to trade in 1853, the flag became an important national symbol. It was officially adopted in 1870 after the Meiji Restoration.

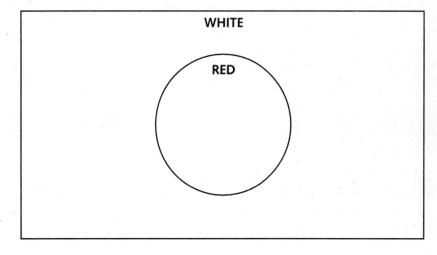

Use after reading Chapter 18, Lesson 1, pages 507–511.

HOW TO TELL PRIMARY FROM SECONDARY SOURCES

Apply Thinking Skills

DIRECTIONS: Read the excerpt from Otto von Bismarck's speech. Then answer the questions that follow.

"Germany does not look to Prussia's liberalism, but to its power. . . . Not by speeches and decisions of majorities will the greatest problems of the times be decided . . . but by iron and blood." *(from a speech delivered by Bismarck to the Prussian legislature on September 30, 1862)*

1. Is the quote from Bismarck a primary or secondary source? Explain your answer.

primary, because it is part of a speech delivered by Bismarck
_____

_____

2. What do you think Bismarck meant by these words? Accept all responses that students
_____

can reasonably defend—for example, Bismarck believed that Prussia must be militarily strong.

_____

3. If a soldier in Bismarck's army wrote a letter home describing a battle that he fought

in, would the letter be a primary or a secondary source? primary _____

_____

4. If a newspaper reporter used the soldier's letter and interviews with people who saw the battle to write an article about the war, would the article be a primary or a

secondary source? secondary _____

_____

5. If someone who observed a meeting of Bismarck and some of his officers made a painting of the meeting, would the painting be a primary or a secondary source?

primary
_____

_____

Use after reading Chapter 18, Skill Lesson, pages 512–513.

Harcourt Brace School Publishers

David Livingstone
EXPLORES AFRICA

Map Skill *Locate Places on a Map*

DIRECTIONS: Read the following statements about Doctor Livingstone's exploration of Africa. Then look at the map on the next page. On it, underline the towns and villages visited by Livingstone. Circle the lakes he visited, and trace over the rivers on which he traveled.

1. Livingstone arrived in Africa at Algoa Bay. He journeyed about 1,000 miles north to Linyante, where he developed close ties with the Makololo tribe.

2. He left Linyante in 1853 and traveled northwest on the Zambezi River. Then he traveled to Lake Dilolo.

3. After returning to Linyante, he left again in 1855. This time he followed the Chobe River northeast to the Zambezi River. Then he traveled east along the Zambezi River, and saw waterfalls that he named Victoria Falls.

4. He continued along the Zambezi River for about 800 miles until he reached the coast near Quelimane, on the Mozambique Channel.

5. Livingstone explored northward along the Shire River and Lake Nyasa. He also explored Lake Tanganyika. He was resting at the village of Ujiji on the northeastern side of the lake when an American, Henry Morton Stanley, found him on November 10, 1871, proving to the world that rumors of Livingstone's death were false.

6. Livingstone died in 1873 in Chitambo village at the southern end of Lake Bangweulu.

Harcourt Brace School Publishers

(Continued)

LIVINGSTONE'S EXPLORATIONS

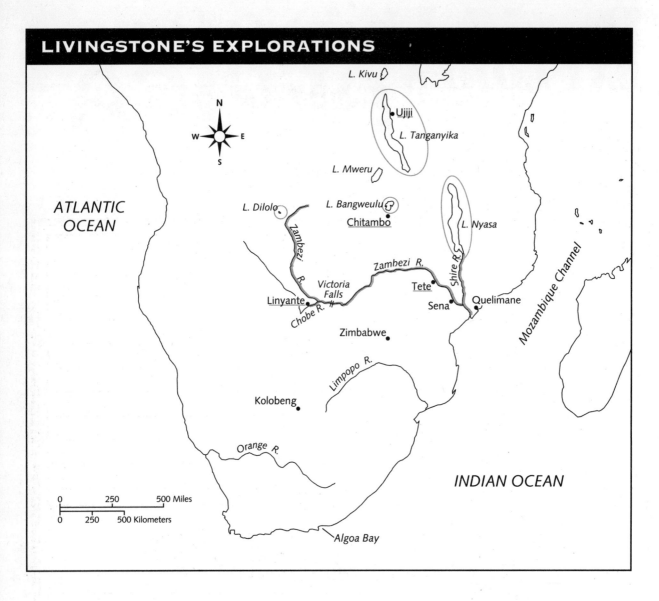

ATLANTIC OCEAN

L. Kivu

Ujiji

L. Tanganyika

L. Mweru

L. Dilolo

L. Bangweulu

Chitambo

L. Nyasa

Zambezi R.

Zambezi R.

Victoria Falls

Shire R.

Tete

Sena

Quelimane

Linyante

Chobe R.

Zimbabwe

Mozambique Channel

Limpopo R.

Kolobeng

Orange R.

INDIAN OCEAN

0   250   500 Miles
0   250   500 Kilometers

Algoa Bay

Use after reading Chapter 18, Lesson 2, pages 514–519.

Growth of Nationalism and Imperialism

Connect Main Ideas

DIRECTIONS: Use the organizer to show that you understand how the chapter's main ideas are connected. Complete the organizer by writing three details for each main idea.

Rise of Nationalism

People in the 1800s developed more of a sense of belonging to a country.

1. Italy: the Red Shirts, or the Young Italy movement; the uniting of various states and nations into one Italy; Mazzini, Garibaldi, and Cavour. Germany: Otto von Bismarck; the defeat of Austria and Denmark; a loose alliance becoming the German Empire; Kaiser Wilhelm.

2. Japan: the army; concern about threats from other countries; the overthrow of the shogun and the reestablishment of the emperor; "Eastern way, Western science."

3. _____

Growth of Nationalism and Imperialism

Age of Imperialism

The Western industrial nations claimed colonies in Africa and Asia

1. Students should include as key ideas that Africa and Asia were seen as sources of raw materials and markets for manufactured goods, European nations divided up Africa, governments conquered lands where companies were doing business, and Western nations

2. felt it was their duty to bring their way of life to the "less-fortunate" peoples of Africa and Asia.

3. _____

Patriotic Posters

Interpret Documents

DIRECTIONS: Study the two World War I posters below.
Then complete the activities that follow.

1. Each poster is trying to appeal to the patriotic spirit of the American people. Circle the words on each poster that tell Americans what they can do to support the war effort.

2. Why do you think doing these things would help the war effort?

Left: eating less food at home meant more food was available to send to allied troops;

Right: Working fast and efficiently in the American factories meant sending much needed supplies

to the troops faster.

3. What do you think the soldier in the first poster might be thinking about?

Accept answers that students can logically defend, e.g. how to stay alive, his family and friends,

etc.

Use after reading Chapter 19, Lesson 1, pages 535–541.

HOW TO USE A Time Zone Map

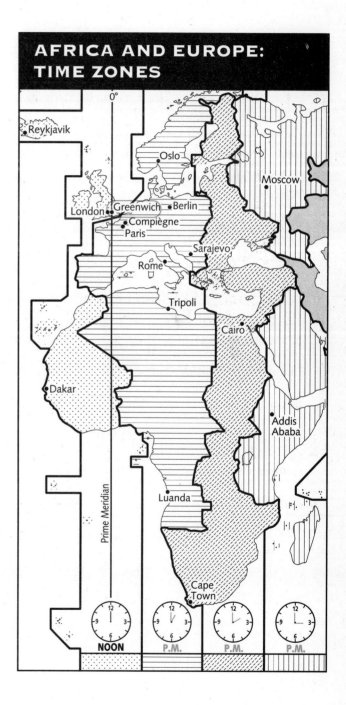

Apply Map Skills

    DIRECTIONS: Study the time zone map to the right. Then complete the activities on page 130.

AFRICA AND EUROPE: TIME ZONES

Reykjavik
Oslo
Moscow
London
Greenwich
Berlin
Compiègne
Paris
Sarajevo
Rome
Tripoli
Cairo
Dakar
Addis Ababa
Prime Meridian
Luanda
Cape Town

NOON P.M. P.M. P.M.

(Continued)

NAME _____ DATE _____

1. Circle Greenwich, England. What is its longitude? 0° _____

2. Draw hands on the clocks to show the correct time in each time zone when it is 12:00 noon at the Prime Meridian. Label the clocks as A.M. or P.M.

3. How many times zones are shown on this map? 4 _____

4. When it is noon at the Prime Meridian, what time is it in Moscow?

3:00 P.M. _____

5. When it is 10:00 P.M. in Cape Town, what time is it in Cairo? 10:00 P.M. _____

6. When it is 1:00 A.M. in Oslo, what time is it in Dakar? 12:00 midnight _____

7. When it is 5:00 P.M. in Addis Ababa, what time is it in Luanda?

3:00 P.M. _____

8. Why don't the time zones precisely match degrees of longitude?

Because some countries have decided to keep the same time throughout all of the country. _____

9. The German delegates at Compiègne, France, worked out the details of the final armistice, or the agreement to stop warfare, of World War I on November 11, 1918. It called for a cease fire on the Western Front at November 11 at 11:00 A.M.—the eleventh hour of the eleventh day of the eleventh month. What time was it in the following cities when the cease fire began?

London, England: _____ 10:00 A.M. _____

Sarajevo, Bosnia: _____ 11:00 A.M. _____

Paris, France: _____ 11:00 A.M. _____

Berlin, Germany: _____ 11:00 A.M. _____

Rome, Italy: _____ 11:00 A.M. _____

Moscow, Russia: _____ 1:00 P.M. _____

Harcourt Brace School Publishers

THE RUSSIAN REVOLUTION

Identify Historical Events and People

DIRECTIONS: Use the following clues to complete the word puzzle. The letters in the box spell out the former name for St. Petersburg, a name which honored a major leader of the Russian Revolution. When filling in the answers, leave spaces between words blank.

1. People who followed Lenin were known as _____.

2. The Communist party formed a secret police force called the _____.

3. _____ took over the job of running the Soviet Union when Lenin died.

4. People who opposed the Bolsheviks put together a force called the _____.

5. Under the rule of Joseph Stalin, the Soviet Union became a _____ state.

6. _____ ruled Russia from 1682 to 1725.

7. Socialism, which led to communism, was the idea of _____.

8. Before the Russian Revolution, Russia was ruled by leaders called _____.

9. Rasputin had influence over _____.

1. B O L S H E V I K S

2. C H E K A

3. J O S E P H ■ S T A L I N

4. W H I T E ■ A R M Y

5. T O T A L I T A R I A N

6. P E T E R ■ T H E ■ G R E A T

7. K A R L ■ M A R X

8. C Z A R S

9. C Z A R I N A ■ A L E X A N D R A

The Early 1900s

Sequence Events

DIRECTIONS: On the line provided, write the year in which each of the following events took place.

A. _____1935_____ Social Security Act passed

B. _____1917_____ Russian Revolution takes place

C. _____1933_____ Hitler becomes chancellor of Germany

D. _____1919_____ Treaty of Versailles signed

E. _____1924_____ Joseph Stalin becomes ruler of Soviet Union

F. _____1917_____ German submarines attack U.S. merchant ships

G. _____1922_____ Russia renamed the Union of Soviet Socialist Republics

H. _____1914_____ Archduke Francis Ferdinand assassinated

DIRECTIONS: Place the letter of each of the above events at the appropriate place on the time line below. If the event was a cause of World War I, or if it took place during World War I, place the letter on the top half of the time line. Place the letters of the other events on the bottom half of the time line.

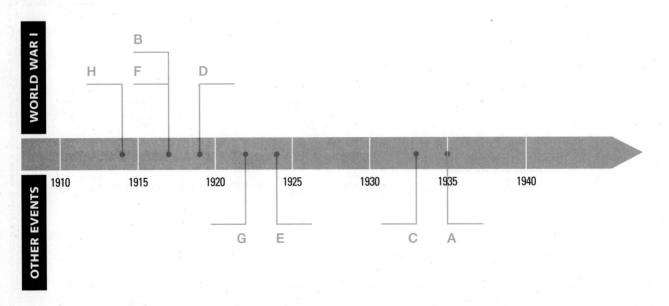

Harcourt Brace School Publishers

The Early Twentieth Century

Connect Main Ideas

DIRECTIONS: Use this organizer to show that you understand how the chapter's main ideas are connected. Complete the organizer by writing three details to support each main idea.

World War 1
Alliances of nations led to World War I.

1. Students may mention reasons why _____ European nations formed alliances, the
2. members of the alliances, the spark that _____ set the alliances against one another,
3. and the effects of that spark. _____

The Russian Revolution
The Russian government changed, yet stayed much the same after the Russian revolution of 1917.

1. Students may mention that a _____ communist government eventually
2. came about and that it promised more _____ to the peasants and workers, but that
3. in reality most Russians still had _____ few rights.

The Early Twentieth Century

The Great Depression
An economic crisis led to the Great Depression and affected countries around the world.

1. Students may mention the underlying reasons for the Great Depression, the stock _____
2. market crash, and the effects of the crash on different parts of the world. _____
3. _____

Use after reading Chapter 19, pages 534–555.

HIDING ANNE FRANK

This diagram shows the Secret Annex at 263 Prinsengracht, Amsterdam, the Netherlands, where the Frank family hid. Otto Frank's offices were on the first and second floor, and storage space was on the third and fourth floors. The Secret Annex was hidden behind the storage space. It was not visible from the road.

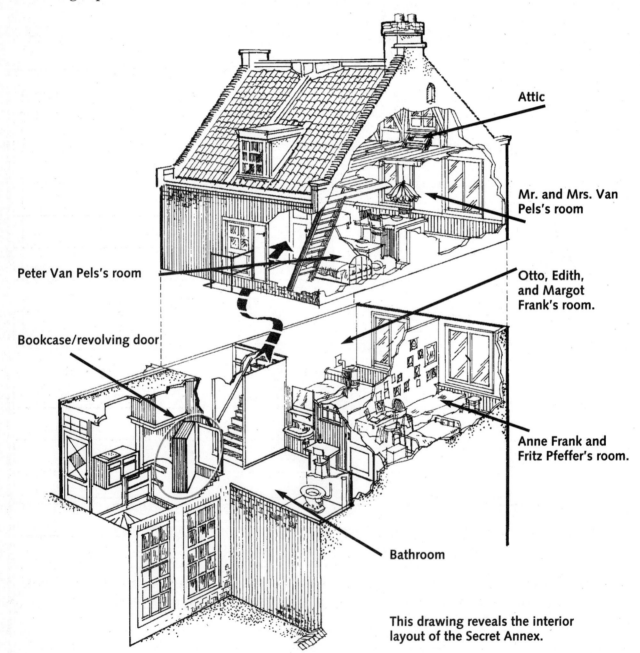

Attic

Mr. and Mrs. Van Pels's room

Peter Van Pels's room

Otto, Edith, and Margot Frank's room.

Bookcase/revolving door

Anne Frank and Fritz Pfeffer's room.

Bathroom

This drawing reveals the interior layout of the Secret Annex.

(Continued)

NAME _____ DATE _____

Interpret a Diagram

**DIRECTIONS: Study the diagram that shows where Anne Frank hid in Amsterdam.
Then use the diagram and your textbook to complete the activities that follow.**

1. The diagram on page 134 shows the Secret Annex where the Frank family hid.
On which floors of the office building was the Secret Annex located?

third and fourth floors

_____

2. Circle the only passageway that led to the Secret Annex.

3. On July 6, 1942, Anne, her father Otto, her mother Edith, and her sister Margot went
into hiding in the Secret Annex. Later, four other friends of the Franks went into hiding
with them. What were the names of these friends? Mr. and Mrs. Van Pels, Peter Van Pels,

and Fritz Pfeffer

4. Why was the Frank family in hiding? The Franks were Jews, and they were hiding to escape

from the Germans.

_____

5. How many rooms were in the Frank family's living area? 3 _____

6. What do you think the attic was used for? storage; exercising; place to be alone

7. What do you think the Frank family did to the windows on the day they arrived

in the Secret Annex? Accept all answers that refer to covering the windows to remain hidden.

You may wish to tell students that in Anne Frank's diary, she describes the making of window

coverings and explains that ". . . these works of art are fixed in position with drawing pins not

to come down until we emerge from here."

_____

8. Anne Frank kept a diary of her life in hiding. Her last entry is August 1, 1944. On a
separate sheet of paper, write five diary entries describing what you think Anne Frank
might have been feeling and thinking while she lived in the Secret Annex.

Student entries should fall between July 6, 1942, and August 1, 1944

HOW TO USE A
Double-Bar Graph

Apply Graph Skills

DIRECTIONS: Study the double-bar graph comparing U.S. casualties in the two world wars. Then complete the activities that follow.

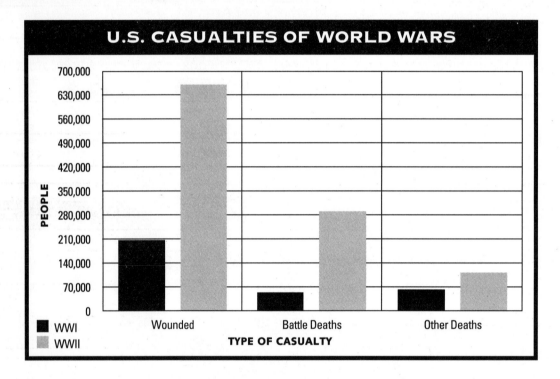

1. How many American soldiers were wounded during WWI? <u>about 210,000</u>

2. How many American soldiers were wounded during WWII? <u>about 650,000</u>

3. During which world war did the United States' military have fewer battle deaths than other deaths? <u>WWI</u>

4. Which world war was more destructive for the United States? Explain your answer.

<u>WWII; Accept any answers that mention the number of wounded and dead, longer time period of</u>

<u>U.S. involvement in war, or more technologically advanced warfare.</u>

_____

_____

Use after reading Chapter 20, Skill Lesson, pages 564–565.

NAME _____ DATE _____

NUMBER THE STARS

Complete an Illustrated Story Map

DIRECTIONS: Complete the following illustrated story map to visually outline Number the Stars by Lois Lowry.

Characters

Annemarie Johansen,

Ellen Rosen, Mama

(Mrs. Johansen),

Papa (Mr. Johansen),

three Nazi

soldiers

Problem and/or goal of the story

How to protect Ellen

from the Nazis

_____

_____

_____

_____

Setting

Where? Johansen apartment in

Nazi-occupied territory

When? 4 A.M. during Holocaust

_____

Event 1

Nazi soldiers knock on

door looking for Rosen

family; begin searching

Johansen apartment.

_____

_____

Event 2

Annemarie yanks

off Ellen's necklace

with Star of David.

Event 3

Soldiers question

children and parents

about Ellen's belonging

to the family.

_____

_____

Event 4

Mr. Johansen shows soldiers

photos of his daughters,

including one of a child

who died.

Resolution

Soldiers believe photo of dead child

shows Ellen; leave apartment; Ellen is

safe for time being.

_____

_____

NAME _____ DATE _____

Who Said What???

Link People with Comments

DIRECTIONS: *Read the statements on the left. Then draw a line from each statement to the name of the person on the right who might have made the statement. The names of some people are used more than once, and some names are not used at all.*

1. My government in Cuba now has close ties with the Soviet Union.

2. We're eyeball to eyeball, and I think the other fellow just blinked.

3. The United States will give money and supplies to any nation trying to resist communism.

4. An iron curtain has descended across the Continent.

5. I refuse to withdraw troops from West Berlin.

6. With the help of China and the Soviet Union, I built a communist state in North Vietnam.

7. As President, I refused to allow U.S. teams to play in the 1980 Summer Olympics as a protest against the Soviet invasion of Afghanistan.

8. I fought against the French to gain independence for my country.

9. I wanted to keep the conflict in Korea from spreading, so I recommended fighting a limited war there.

10. Peaceful coexistence among different systems of government is possible.

Adolf Hitler

Dean Rusk

Fidel Castro

Harry Truman

Ho Chi Minh

Jimmy Carter

John F. Kennedy

Joseph Stalin

Nikita Khrushchev

Winston Churchill

Use after reading Chapter 20, Lesson 3, pages 572–578.

HOW TO MAKE A
Thoughtful Decision

Apply Thinking Skills

DIRECTIONS: *Think about an event that will take place at your school this week. Use the organizer below to record and analyze your thoughts about that event. Then decide what you think should happen.*

THE GOAL

Students should choose an event that will occur at school this week. Example: A school club plans to hand out a flyer showing a map of the countries of the world

POSSIBLE SHORT-TERM CONSEQUENCES

Students should include both positive and negative consequences.

Input

POSSIBLE LONG-TERM CONSEQUENCES

Students should include both positive and negative consequences.

THINK AND APPLY

1. Write a plus sign (+) next to each consequence that is positive and a negative sign (−) next to each one that is negative.

2. Count the number of positive signs. _____
   Count the number of negative signs. _____

   Students should place positive and negative signs next to all positive and negative consequences.

3. Did you have more negative or positive signs? _____

YOU DECIDE

Given the positive and negative consequences of this event, do you think it should take place as scheduled? Or, do you think you should suggest making changes in the event based on the consequences?

_____

_____

_____

The Later Twentieth Century

Connect Main Ideas

DIRECTIONS: Use this organizer to show that you understand how the chapter's main ideas are connected. Complete the organizer by writing several sentences to describe each of the following topics.

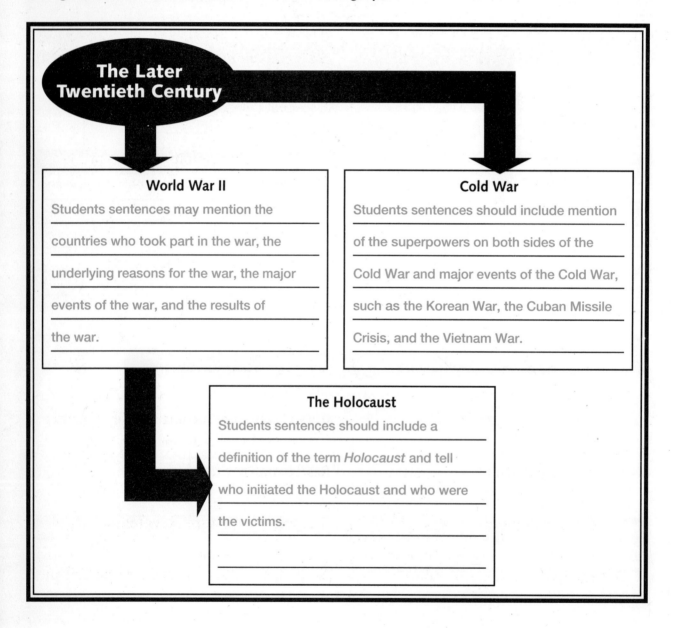

The Later Twentieth Century

World War II

Students sentences may mention the

countries who took part in the war, the

underlying reasons for the war, the major

events of the war, and the results of

the war.

Cold War

Students sentences should include mention

of the superpowers on both sides of the

Cold War and major events of the Cold War,

such as the Korean War, the Cuban Missile

Crisis, and the Vietnam War.

The Holocaust

Students sentences should include a

definition of the term *Holocaust* and tell

who initiated the Holocaust and who were

the victims.

Harcourt Brace School Publishers

Use after reading Chapter 20, pages 556–581.

Influences on
CHINESE HISTORY

Connect Causes and Their Effects

DIRECTIONS: The statements in the left column below identify some causes that resulted in changes in Chinese history. The right column lists effects of these changes. Draw a line from each cause to its effect on the right.

CAUSES	EFFECTS
1. Foreign influences on China	Mao Zedong's widow put in jail
2. Refusal of warlords to follow orders of Nationalist government	Discovery of leadership qualities of Mao Zedong
3. Ability to defeat warlords	Split in Nationalist party
4. Desire of peasants to have more say in government	Rise of People's Nationalist party
5. Long March	Formation of the Red Guard
6. Mao Zedong defeats Nationalists	End of Cultural Revolution
7. Mao Zedong displeased with failure of Chinese to follow his ideas	Chiang Kai-shek becomes leader of China
8. Moderates gain control	Resignation of Sun Yat-sen
9. Cultural Revolution	Beginning of Cultural Revolution
10. Destruction of Chinese economy	Beginning of Republic of China on Taiwan

HOW TO READ a Cartogram

CARTOGRAM OF ASIA IN 2010: PROJECTED POPULATION

Countries shown by number

1 UNITED ARAB EMIRATES
2 QATAR
3 BAHRAIN
4 KUWAIT
5 JORDAN
6 LEBANON
7 ISRAEL
8 ARMENIA
9 AZERBAIJAN
10 TURKMENISTAN

11 UZBEKISTAN
12 AFGHANISTAN
13 TAJIKISTAN
14 KYRGYZSTAN
15 CAMBODIA
16 MACAO
17 HONG KONG

MONGOLIA

CHINA

NORTH KOREA

SOUTH KOREA

JAPAN

KAZAKSTAN

GEORGIA

TURKEY

8 9

11

13 14

12

10

SAUDI ARABIA

IRAN

PAKISTAN

IRAQ

SYRIA

YEMEN   OMAN

6

7 5

3 4

1 2

BHUTAN

NEPAL

INDIA

BANGLADESH

BURMA (MYANMAR)

LAOS

THAILAND

VIETNAM

16 17

15

BRUNEI

MALAYSIA

SINGAPORE

TAIWAN

PHILIPPINES

INDONESIA

MALDIVES

SRI LANKA

(Continued)

Use after reading Chapter 21, Skill Lesson, pages 598–599.

Harcourt Brace School Publishers

Apply Map Skills

DIRECTIONS: Review the cartogram on page 142. Then compare it to the political map of Asia and Europe on pages A8 and A9 of your textbook. Check the box before each statement below that applies to the cartogram or political map. Some statements may apply to both.

CARTOGRAM	POLITICAL MAP	STATEMENT
	√	Shows countries in correct geographic location
	√	Identifies major bodies of water
√		Provides population information
	√	Shows exact location of countries
	√	Shows correct sizes of countries
	√	Shows correct shapes of countries
√	√	Shows all the countries of Asia

DIRECTIONS: Use either the cartogram on page 142 or the political map of Asia and Europe on pages A8 and A9 of your textbook to answer the questions below. In the space to the left of each question, write a C if you found the answer on the cartogram or a P if you found the answer on the political map.

1. __P__ What is the capital of Indonesia? _Jakarta_____

2. __P__ What river system in Iraq empties into the Persian Gulf? _Tigris-Euphrates___

3. __C__ What country is expected to be the most populated country in Asia in 2010?
   _China_____

4. __P__ Is Indonesia south or north of India? _south_____

5. __P__ Describe the shape of Sri Lanka. _It is shaped like a teardrop._____

6. __C__ Will North Korea or South Korea have more people in 2010?
   _South Korea_____

7. __P__ Which is the largest country in Asia? _China_____

8. __P__ What body of water separates Japan from the mainland of Asia?
   _the Sea of Japan_____

9. __C__ If about 100 million people will live in Iran in 2010, about how many people do you
   think will live in South Korea? _50 million_____

Harcourt Brace School Publishers

BALANCE of TRADE

Hypothesize from Information in a Table

DIRECTIONS: The table below shows the balance of trade between the United States and some of its major trading partners in Asia. A minus (−) sign indicates a negative balance of trade. A positive (+) sign indicates a positive balance of trade. Examine the table. Then answer the questions that follow.

TRADING PARTNER	1989	1990	1991	1992	1993
China	−6,235	−10,431	−12,691	−18,309	−22,768
Hong Kong	−3,431	−2,805	−1,142	−716	+315
India	−857	−711	−1,194	−1,863	−1,790
Indonesia	−2,282	−1,444	−1,349	−1,750	−2,669
Japan	−49,051	−41,105	−43,386	−49,601	−59,319
Philippines	−866	−913	−1,206	−1,597	−1,367
Singapore	−1,658	−1,778	−1,153	−1,687	−1,120
South Korea	−6,278	−4,081	−1,514	−2,043	−2,347
Taiwan	−12,978	−11,175	−9,841	−9,346	−8,855
Thailand	−2,091	−2,293	−2,369	−3,540	−4,774
Numbers are in millions of U.S. dollars					

SOURCE: U.S. Statistical Abstracts, 1994, page 823

1. In the table above, circle the name of the trading partner with which the United States had the largest negative balance of trade for every year shown.

2. Draw a line under the name of the trading partner with which the United States had a positive balance of trade in 1993.

3. Would you expect the U.S. balance of trade with Taiwan to be higher or lower in 1994? _lower_____

4. Would you expect the U.S. balance of trade with China to be higher or lower in 1994? _higher_____

5. What products do you think explain the negative balance of trade with Japan?
automobiles, electronic equipment

Use after reading Chapter 21, Lesson 2, pages 600–604.

Harcourt Brace School Publishers

HOW TO READ a Climograph

Apply Graph Skills

DIRECTIONS: Using the information in the table below, complete the climograph that follows.

HONG KONG												
	JAN	**FEB**	**MAR**	**APRIL**	**MAY**	**JUNE**	**JULY**	**AUG**	**SEP**	**OCT**	**NOV**	**DEC**
Temperature	60	59	63	71	78	81	82	82	81	77	69	63
Precipitation	1.3	1.8	2.9	5.4	11.5	15.5	15.0	14.2	10.1	4.5	1.7	1.2

Temperatures are given in degrees (°) Fahrenheit. Precipitation information is given in inches.

DIRECTIONS: Compare the climograph of Hong Kong with the climograph of Tokyo on page 605 of your textbook. Then answer the questions that follow.

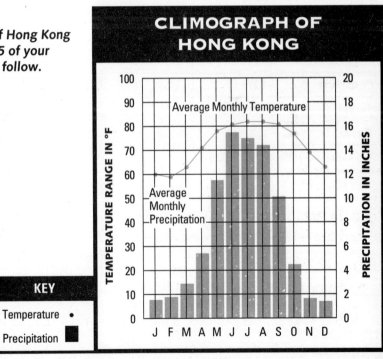

1. Which city has the warmer summer? _Hong Kong_____

2. Which city has the drier summer? _Tokyo_____

3. During which season of the year does Hong Kong receive the most rainfall?

_summer_____

Which Country Am I?

Identify Countries in South America

DIRECTIONS: Color the flag of each country below as appropriate. Then read the statements that follow. In the blank to the left of each statement, write the correct letter of the country that the statement describes.

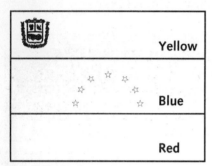

Yellow

Blue

Red

A. Venezuela

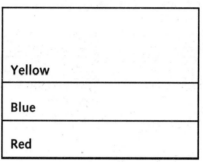

Yellow

Blue

Red

B. Colombia

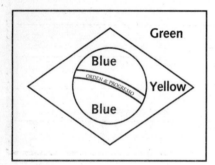

Green

Blue

ORDEN & PROGRESSO

Yellow

Blue

C. Brazil

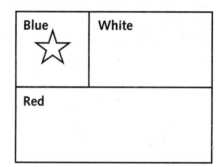

Blue

White

Red

D. Chile

C
_____ **1.** I am the most heavily industrialized country in South America. I export a variety of products such as bananas, cacao, and beef.

D
_____ **2.** I have a dry climate in the north, where the Atacama Desert is located.

A
_____ **3.** I am the home of the world's highest waterfall.

D
_____ **4.** My main source of income is copper.

A
_____ **5.** Oil is my main export, and it made me rich during the 1970s and 1980s.

D
_____ **6.** I was ruled by Salvador Allende, who changed the economy from a free-enterprise economy to a socialist economy.

B
_____ **7.** Coffee makes up about half of my exports.

C
_____ **8.** Careless development of my natural resources has caused a huge problem for Amazonia.

Use after reading Chapter 21, Lesson 3, pages 606–611.

Harcourt Brace School Publishers

Free Trade

Link History to Geography

DIRECTIONS: *Study the map on page 619 in your textbook. Write the names of the countries in each trade group in the appropriate column in the chart below. Then write an N next to the countries that are located in North America and an S next to the countries that are located in South America.*

FREE-TRADE GROUPS IN NORTH AND SOUTH AMERICA

NORTH AMERICAN FREE TRADE AGREEMENT (NAFTA)	LATIN AMERICAN FREE TRADE ASSOCIATION (LAFTA)		CENTRAL AMERICAN COMMON MARKET
Canada N	Argentina S	Ecuador S	Costa Rica N
United States N	Bolivia S	Paraguay S	El Salvador N
Mexico N	Brazil S	Peru S	Guatemala N
	Chile S	Uruguay S	Honduras N
	Colombia S	Venezuela S	Mexico N
			Nicaragua N
			Panama N

DIRECTIONS: *Use your completed chart above and the map on page 619 in your textbook to answer the following questions.*

1. What is the name of the largest country that is a member of NAFTA?

Canada

2. What country is a member of both NAFTA and the Central American Common Market?

Mexico

3. Why do you think some small areas of South America are not part of LAFTA?

Because these areas are not independent countries

4. Why do you think North American countries are not part of LAFTA?

For now the organization is limited to South American countries only.

Use after reading Chapter 21, Lesson 4, pages 614–619.

Harcourt Brace School Publishers

ECONOMIC CHALLENGES

Connect Main Ideas

DIRECTIONS: Use this organizer to show that you understand how the chapter's main ideas are connected. Complete the organizer by writing several sentences to describe the economic challenges the different countries have faced in the twentieth century.

China

Students' sentences may mention the need to modernize; China's five-year plans; the failure of the Great Leap Forward; the cultural revolution that destroyed China's economy; and Deng Xiaoping's Four Modernizations with the reintroduction of free enterprise into the economy.

Japan

Students may include the destruction of Japan's economy during World War II and the need for Japan to rebuild; the economic miracle, with help from the United States; Japan's few natural resources and dependence on foreign oil supplies; competition from other Asian nations.

Economic Challenges

The Countries of South America

Students' answers may include the colonial legacy of single product economies; the great debt; the vast difference between rich and poor people's lifeways; developing nations.

The Countries of North America

Students may mention that Canada struggles with inflation, unemployment, and the desire by many French Canadians to have a separate nation; Mexico's economy is highly dependent on oil refining and has a high national debt. The United States economy is in transition from a manufacturing base to a service base, faces inflation, national debt, and high government spending.

Harcourt Brace School Publishers

Use after reading Chapter 21, pages 592–621.

INDIAN WORD SCRAMBLE

Identify Indian History

DIRECTIONS: Use the clues on the right to help you unscramble the words on the left. Write the unscrambled words in the space provided.

MOHANDAS GANDHI

NOSADMAH GAHIND _____

SATYAGRAHA

AHATRASGYA _____

JAWAHARLAL NEHRU

HALJARALAW RENUH _____

MUHAMMAD ALI JINNAH

HUMDAMAM LIA NIHJAN _____

MAHATMA GANDHI

ATHAMAM HIDAGN _____

INDIRA GANDHI

DNAIRI DAGHIN _____

BENAZIR BHUTTO

NEIRBAZ THTOBU _____

KASHMIR

MIKRHAS _____

BANGLADESH

AHBGASNDEL _____

HARIJANS

AIJRNASH _____

1. A young Indian lawyer who became a strong leader of India

2. Bad actions are paid back by good ones

3. Appointed by Britain to lead India to independence

4. Muslim leader of Northern Indian independence movement

5. The leader who was renamed "Great Soul"

6. Murdered by the Sikhs

7. Prime minister of Pakistan

8. Struggle over this area brought India and Pakistan to war

9. Gained independence in 1971

10. Gandhi's name for the untouchables

Harcourt Brace School Publishers

HOW TO USE Different Types of Population Maps

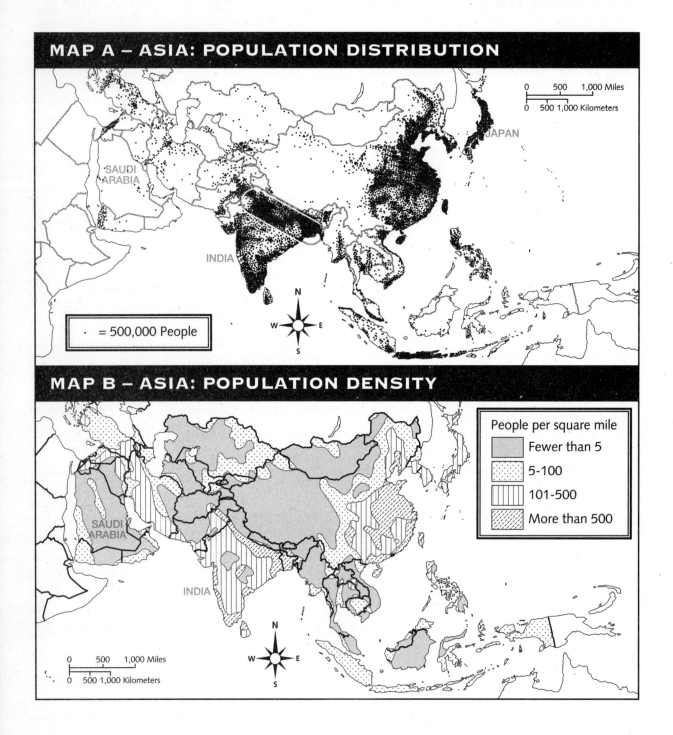

MAP A – ASIA: POPULATION DISTRIBUTION

0   500   1,000 Miles
0 500 1,000 Kilometers

JAPAN

SAUDI ARABIA

INDIA

· = 500,000 People

N
W   E
S

MAP B – ASIA: POPULATION DENSITY

People per square mile
Fewer than 5
5-100
101-500
More than 500

SAUDI ARABIA

INDIA

0   500   1,000 Miles
0 500 1,000 Kilometers

N
W   E
S

Harcourt Brace School Publishers

(Continued)

Apply Map Skills

DIRECTIONS: Study the two maps on page 150. Both show population density. The top map shows density using dots. The bottom map uses different patterns to show different levels of population density. Use these two maps to complete the activities below.

1. Label Japan on Map A. How would you describe the distribution of dots in Japan?

There are so many of them that most of the country is solid black.

2. Find Japan on Map B. What is the population density for most of the country?

101–500 people per square mile

3. Which area of Asia is most densely populated? Least densely populated?

Explain your answers. Most: coastlines; least: interior; accept answers that refer to the climate,

access to water, and historical development of country.

4. Label Saudi Arabia on Map B. What is the population density of most of Saudi Arabia?

fewer than 5 people per square mile

5. On Map A, label India. Circle the heavy concentration of dots in northern India. What does this heavy concentration of dots tell you about the population of the area?

that it is very densely populated

6. Find and label India on Map B. What is the population density of the area you circled

on Map A? more than 500 people per square mile

7. What conclusions might you be able to draw about this part of the world based on

its population? Possible responses may include the river valley provides rich farmland,

transportation, and drinking water; and the mild climate.

8. Which map provides the best overall view of where the heaviest population areas are

in Asia? Explain your answer. Map A, because the high density of dots makes some areas look

black, allowing viewer to make the connection that large number of dots equals dense populations.

9. Which map would you use if you wanted to know the specific number of people living in a part of China? Explain your answer.

Map B, because it provides information on the number of people per square mile

Crossroads of Religion

Interpret a Double-Bar Graph

DIRECTIONS: Study the double-bar graph, which shows the three major world religions that began in the Middle East. Then complete the activities below.

1. About how many Christians are there in Asia?

   300,000,000

2. About how many Christians are there in the world?

   1,850,000,000

3. Are there more Christians, Muslims, or Jews in Asia?

   Muslims

4. About how many Jews are there in Asia?

   6,000,000

5. About how many Muslims are there in the world?

   1,000,000,000

6. About how many more Christians than Muslims are there in the world?

   about 850,000,000

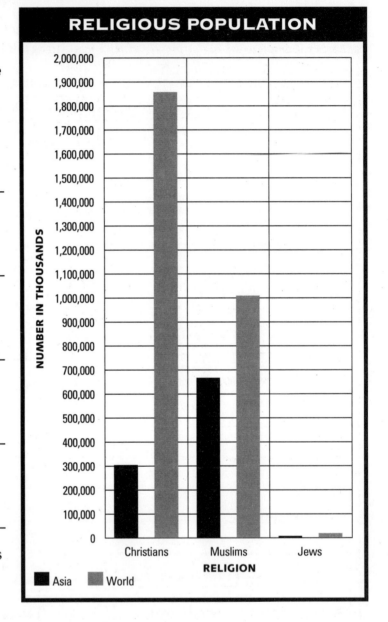

RELIGIOUS POPULATION

7. About how many more Muslims than Christians are there in Asia?

   about 370,000,000

Use after reading Chapter 22, Lesson 2, pages 630–637.

Religious Influences

Connect Main Ideas

DIRECTIONS: Use this organizer to show that you understand how the chapter's main ideas are connected. Complete the organizer by writing three details to support each main idea.

Religious Influences in the Twentieth Century

Indian Subcontinent

Religion has greatly affected the history of the Indian subcontinent.

1. Students may include the conflict between the Hindus and the Muslims in India: there was bloody violence between them when India gained its independence; after independence,

2. India was divided in two—one Muslim country, one Hindu. The Sikhs struggle to survive in India.

3. _____

The Middle East

Ideas and beliefs have both united and divided people in Southwest Asia and North Africa.

1. Details students may include are that three religions grew up in Southwest Asia: Judaism, Islam, and Christianity; both Jews and Muslims claim Abraham as their ancestor; Arab nationalism and

2. common religion have unified an Arab alliance against Israel, which has a different religion; Islamic renewal; OPEC and the PLO are instances of unity among the Muslims of Southwest Asia

3. and North Africa.

Harcourt Brace School Publishers

Use SWAHILI NUMBERS

Apply Other Languages

DIRECTIONS: The table below provides the Swahili words for English numbers one through ten. Read each of the statements that follow the table. Determine how many examples are provided in each statement. Then, on the line provided, write the Swahili word for that number.

ENGLISH NUMBER	SWAHILI NUMBER	PRONUNCIATION
one	moja	MO•jah
two	mbili	mm•BEE•lee
three	tatu	TAH•too
four	nne	NN•nay
five	tano	TAH•no
six	sita	SEE•tah
seven	saba	SAH•bah
eight	nane	NAH•nay
nine	tisa	TEE•sah
ten	kumi	KOO•mee

_____tano_____ **1.** The San people of the Kalahari Desert use simple tools such as the bow, arrow, hook, staff, and spear.

_____saba_____ **2.** Lions, elephants, hippopotamuses, apes, leopards, giraffes, and rhinoceroses are native to Africa.

_____moja_____ **3.** Africa is the Earth's second largest continent.

_____nane_____ **4.** The Nile crocodile, hermit ibis, goliath frog, yeheb nut bush, pygmy hippopotamus, okapi, mountain gorilla, and lemur are all endangered species in Africa.

_____kumi_____ **5.** The Kush, Sheba, Ghana, Mali, Songhay, Yoruba, Bornu, Benin, Ashanti, and Zanj are all peoples that were once part of ancient Africa's great kingdoms.

_____sita_____ **6.** Africa is famous for arts and crafts such as kente cloth, terra-cotta sculptures, bronze figures, masks, woven tapestries, and wood carvings.

_____mbili_____ **7.** Swahili and Afrikaans are examples of African languages.

Use after reading Chapter 23, Lesson 1, pages 641–646.

Journey TO Jo'burg

The story *Journey to Jo'burg* is fiction. The information about South Africa in Lesson 1 is nonfiction. Many fiction books like *Journey to Jo'burg* use make-believe characters to tell a story that includes some historical facts.

Distinguish Fiction from Nonfiction

DIRECTIONS: Decide whether each statement that follows is fiction or nonfiction. Write an F next to each statement of fiction. Write an NF next to each statement of nonfiction.

___NF___ **1.** Apartheid ruled in South Africa for more than 40 years.

___F___ **2.** Naledi, Tiro, and Dineo lived with their grandmother in one of the black homelands.

___NF___ **3.** Under apartheid, black South Africans were forced to live in separate homelands.

___NF___ **4.** Under apartheid, black South Africans had to have permits to live outside of Bantustans.

___NF___ **5.** During the settlement of South Africa, almost all white South Africans held racist views about black South Africans.

___F___ **6.** The mother of Naledi, Tiro, and Dineo worked in Parktown.

___NF___ **7.** Parktown is a suburb of Johannesburg.

___F___ **8.** Naledi and Tiro set off on a bus to find their mother to save their baby sister.

___NF___ **9.** Under apartheid, there were separate buses for whites and for non-whites.

___F___ **10.** Grace Mbatha's mother lived in Soweto.

Global Awareness

Think Globally

DIRECTIONS: In Chapter 23 of your textbook, you have read about many problems and changes that have occurred around the world. For each of the topics below, circle the degree to which you think your own life and the world have been affected by these changes. Circle 1 for very little, 2 for somewhat, and 3 for very much. Student answers will vary.

	YOUR LIFE			THE WORLD		
1. Fall of communism	1	2	3	1	2	3
2. Breakup of apartheid	1	2	3	1	2	3
3. *Perestroika* and *glasnost*	1	2	3	1	2	3
4. Breakup of the Soviet Union	1	2	3	1	2	3
5. Spread of AIDS in Africa	1	2	3	1	2	3
6. Ethnic cleansing in Bosnia	1	2	3	1	2	3
7. Unification of Germany	1	2	3	1	2	3
8. Breakup of Yugoslavia	1	2	3	1	2	3
9. Possible unification of Europe	1	2	3	1	2	3
10. Breakup of Czechoslovakia	1	2	3	1	2	3
11. Drought and famine in Somalia	1	2	3	1	2	3

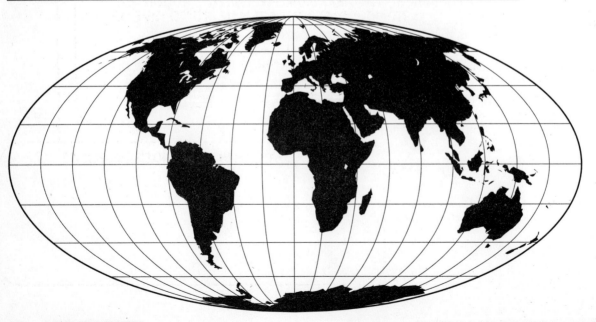

HOW TO RESOLVE Conflicts

Apply Thinking Skills

DIRECTIONS: For each step below, write your arguments for or against a United States of Europe. You may need to write your answers outside the boxes or on a separate sheet of paper.

DECIDE WHAT YOU WANT TO ACHIEVE

Students should choose to work for or against a United States of Europe.

Repeat the first four steps, if compromise is not reached.

DECIDE WHAT YOU ARE WILLING TO GIVE UP

Students should list what they will give up to achieve their goal.

EXPRESS TO THE OTHER SIDE, EITHER ORALLY OR IN WRITING, WHAT YOU ARE WILLING TO GIVE UP

Pair students—those who want to join with those who do not—to exchange papers.

EVALUATE THE OTHER SIDE'S RESPONSE

The students in each pair should evaluate each other's reasons for and against a United States of Europe. Have students repeat the steps of the process to reach a compromise. After each pair has reached a compromise, have students share their findings on the process of compromise with the class.

Harcourt Brace School Publishers

Political Events

Connect Main Ideas

DIRECTIONS: Use this organizer to show that you understand how the chapter's main ideas are connected. Complete the organizer by writing the main idea for each topic.

Political Events

Africa South of the Sahara

Students' answers may cite that colonial

boundaries separated people of the same

ethnic group and included peoples of rival

ethnic groups; there were some civil wars

after independence; many nations had cash

crop economies so economic recovery and

export diversification have been challenges;

there were totalitarian governments but

now democracy is beginning to spread;

droughts and famines have occurred.

Eastern Europe and Russia

Students may mention that perestroika and

glasnost gave Soviet republics the freedom

to call for independence; Eastern European

countries also wanted more freedom;

the Soviet Union stayed out of their

independence movements; East and West

Germany reunited; there is now democracy

in the former Soviet Union; with the

independence of the Balkans, nationalism

has led to ethnic cleansing.

Use after reading Chapter 23, pages 640–661.